BE MY LOVE

'I'm sorry,' she said.

'Sorry for what, Miranda?'

'Sorry because – oh, please, let me be—' She tried to pull away from him, but still he forced her to look at him.

'Sorry because yesterday I kissed you as if you were a woman?' His voice grew harsher. 'Sorry, Miranda, because you have made me fall in love with you?' She let out a little shuddering sigh of happiness before he kissed her full on the lips, with passion.

This time, she didn't run away.

Also by Daisy Thomson in *Star*

BE MY LOVE

Daisy Thomson

A STAR BOOK
published by
the Paperback Division of
W. H. ALLEN & Co. Ltd

A Star Book
Published in 1977
by the Paperback Division of W. H. Allen & Co. Ltd
A Howard and Wyndham Company
123 King Street, London W6 9JG

First published in Great Britain by
Robert Hale Ltd, 1968

Printed in Great Britain by
Hazell Watson & Viney Ltd, Aylesbury, Bucks

ISBN 0 352 39500 1

Be My Love

Chapter One

An unearthly screech shattered my restful slumber.

I struggled back to consciousness, fighting against the heavy eyed languour to which I had succumbed after climbing high up the mountainside on this hot, oppressive June afternoon, with the echoes of the blood-curdling yell which had roused me still ringing in my ears.

Slowly I sat up, rubbing the sleepiness from my eyes, but now all was quiet, except for the soughing of the wind down among the aromatic pine trees which covered the lower slopes of the Tyrolean hillside below me.

Had I imagined that awful noise? Had it only been part of an unreal nightmare? Once more I rubbed my eyes. Surely I could not have dreamed up that horrifying scream—it had sounded much too real to be a part of unreality.

I blinked and peered about me with fearful gaze.

I was lying in a grassy, gentian strewn hollow, hidden from view of the pathway which skirted the mountainside by a dense, waist-high hedge of pink Alpine rhododendrons, and from view of anyone on higher ground by an overhanging cliff face, and all I myself could see, until I stood up, was this grim, grey expanse of rock, a brilliant wedge of blue sky beyond it, and the rosy pink wall of bloom.

I strained my ears for further sounds, but now

all I could hear was the melancholy murmur of the breeze in the pine tops. There did not seem to be another soul within miles of the little glade where I was sitting; the special, secret glade which Liesl, my Austrian friend whose parents owned the guest-house half-way down the valley, and I had discovered years ago, when we first explored the hillside together.

A cloud passed over the face of the sun, and in the ensuing chill of air, I shivered.

In that moment, I was very much aware of my aloneness. I stretched sideways to get hold of my ski-pants and warm pullover to cover up the brief pink bikini in which I had been sunbathing. Somehow I no longer felt at ease. I wanted to dress and get away from here, down the mountain path, back to the Gasthof, as quickly as I possibly could.

I am a normally sensible young woman of twenty-two, but at this moment, it seemed to me that a sixth sense I had not known I possessed, was warning me to get away from this spot, to escape from some malignant force which was abroad this afternoon on the once more sun-drenched hillside.

As I pulled my gay, pink pullover over my honey brown hair, I tried to shake off this peculiar feeling of unease. Then, as I stood up to pull on my trousers and fasten the zip, I heard another sound which froze the blood coursing through my veins.

From a point only yards away from me came the sound of a man's laugh. It was not a pleasant laugh. It was more a vocal expression of malice, and malice triumphant at that!

While I stood there, my fingers rigid on the pull up of the trouser zip, my whole body as rigid as if it had been sculpted from marble, a man's voice, in the soft accent of Bavaria, spoke in satisfied tones.

"There goes one who will not trouble us again!"

The malicious laugh came again, and a harsher, deeper, more precise voice replied:

"You are quite right, my friend. Dead men tell no tales! I must congratulate you on the quickness of your thinking. When Rudi is found down in the valley below, his death will be accepted as an unfortunate accident. An unfortunate slip on a dangerous path! Who would dream of looking beyond that?"

As I listened in horror to this conversation, I had to bite my lip fiercely to keep my teeth from chattering and so perhaps betray my importunate presence.

Who were these men? Who was the poor devil they had cold-bloodedly pushed to his death? How near were they to the spot where I stood eavesdropping?

Sound carries in odd ways on the high slopes, but I did not doubt these two men were much too near me for comfort. What would they do to me if they spotted me?

That was a question I tried not to answer, as my trembling fingers fastened the button over the zip.

The sound of footsteps scraping harshly on

the loose scree of the overhanging cliff above me galvanized me to more urgent action. I hurriedly bent down, grabbed up my bottle of sun lotion, the paperback I had started to read before drowsiness overcame me, my camera and sunglasses, and stuffed them into my duffle-bag. I snatched up my heavy walking shoes, which I had kicked off when I peeled off my clothes to sunbathe earlier in the afternoon, but not wasting time by trying to put them on, I moved stealthily across the flower starred strip of greensward towards the thickest clump of alpenrosen, and carefully pushed my way into its centre, praying all the time that the faint rustling my action caused would be merged in the sighing of the wind in the treetops below.

Chapter Two

I don't know how long I squatted crouched amongst the scented shrubs.

It could have been ten minutes, half an hour, or eternity, while I waited for the men on the escarpment overhead to come walking down the pathway which passed so close to my hiding place, for this path was the only safe way down to the valley, unless one was very familiar with the Schwarzberg, and even with familiarity, it was not always wise to choose another way, since frequent landslides and late spring avalanches altered the topographical features of these high alps from day to day.

At last they came. Now I could hear the grating of studded walking shoes on the loose gravel of the footway which led down the mountainside.

Nearer and nearer came the sound, and now the men were so close I could have put out a hand and touched them as they passed, but for all their closeness, the foliage concealing me was fortunately so thick that I could not even catch a glimpse of them, a fact which reassured me, for if I could not see them, knowing they were there, they certainly would never suspect my presence!

As they clambered past, one of the men was whistling softly to himself. The tune was vaguely familiar, although I could not put a name to it, but the whistler's rendering was slightly off key, which did not help in the identification.

Gradually the sound of footsteps faded, but still I waited, crouched uncomfortably amongst the sharp twigs which cut into my bare feet, and with heaven knew what strange spiders and other insects crawling ticklishly through my hair and alarmingly exploring the nape of my neck. I grew colder and more cramped, but I allowed a considerable time to elapse before I thought it safe to emerge from hiding.

I pulled on my shoes, tied the laces firmly, and started a cautious descent of the path.

I was constantly on the alert, ready to dive for cover if I saw anyone on the mountain, but I reached the shelter of the belt of pine trees without seeing a single soul. Here I felt safe for the first time for over an hour, and I hurried along the pathway which led to the Gasthof feeling almost giddy with relief, but it was not until I stepped from the deep shade of the woodland path into the bright sunshine of the lower valley that warmth returned to my body.

I was still nervy, however, because when Niall Paterson, a fellow guest at the Schwarzberghof, called out from behind me as I joined the main pathway, I started violently.

"Hey, there!" exclaimed Niall, as his long strides took him alongside me. "What on earth have you been up to, Miranda? You look as if you had come from an encounter with a ghost!"

It was on the tip of my tongue to tell Niall all about my terrifying experience on the Schwarzberg, but before I could find the words to do so, he went on,

"You look as if you had a nasty fall," he observed. "There is a rip right down the back of your pullover, and it is filthy with leaves and twigs. Is that what upset you?"

I quickly swallowed back the truth.

On my way back down the mountain path, after much thought I had decided not to mention what I had heard, although I had very nearly gone back on my resolve and blurted out the truth at Niall's unexpected question. What I had told myself was that there was no sense in my involving myself in something which did not concern me.

After all, if I went to the police with my story, what good would it do? I could not help them by describing the men who had pushed their companion over the cliff, so what was the use of my contacting them? I would only be needlessly involving myself in criminal proceedings, and I did not know how long these proceedings might last. I could be held up in Austria indefinitely. Stupid, cowardly, selfish, call my reactions what you will, but I decided to say nothing, not even to Niall, of what had happened.

"Yes," I agreed with the young lawyer. "I came a really nasty cropper over a protruding root on the track in the wood. It gave me quite a shake!"

"It most certainly did!" agreed Niall. "You are white as a sheet."

He took my arm and walked with me to the Gasthof.

"I tell you what," he said. as we reached the door of the Inn. "You nip up to your bedroom before your friend Liesl sees the state you are in and starts to fuss over you, and I shall change from my climbing boots and meet you in the bar, where a cognac will soon bring some colour back to your cheeks."

"I shan't be long," I promised, and hurried up to my room, where a quick wash, a change of clothes, a vigorous brushing of twiglets and cobwebs from my hair, and a gay dash of lipstick on my still pallid lips made quite a difference to my appearance.

I went down to join Niall in the dark, woodpanelled parlour bar of the Gasthof.

He was perched on one of the high stools at the bar counter, talking to a tallish, athletic-looking man with untidy dark hair, and face so deeply tanned it made his hazel eyes seem more grey than brown.

"Ah, Miranda! You were quick!" Niall smiled at me with his attractive smile. "Come and meet a fellow-countryman of ours, who arrived at Schwarzberg this afternoon. Mr. Crispin."

He paused, and turning to his companion, continued, "Crispin, this is Miranda MacIntosh, an old friend of Liesl, the daughter of our host; a recent student at Graz University; an authority on the flora of the region; and the fastest girl on four wheels I have ever met!"

I smiled at the stranger.

"Niall should get a job on *Who's Who*, shouldn't he?" I extended my hand.

Crispin took it in a firm clasp, and his eyes

swept over me with such keen interest that I had the uncomfortable feeling he had even noticed the tiny disfiguring scar at the corner of my mouth, the outcome of a bicycle accident in my youth, and a flaw I always do my best to hide under a layer of cosmetics.

I pulled my hand away from his grip and, turning to Niall, asked:

"How about the cognac you promised me?"

"Coming up, Miranda," he smiled, and gave the order to Heinrich, the barman, who had come on duty as Paterson was introducing me to Crispin.

Crispin raised his eyebrows at my choice of drink, and I guessed from his disapproving scowl he did not think a young woman like me should be drinking spirits at this early hour of the afternoon.

Niall, noticing the look, hastily explained:

"Poor Miranda had a nasty fall in the woods a short time ago. When I met her, she looked so shaken I thought she should have something to revive her."

"I tripped over a tree root," the story came glibly to my lips with repetition.

"You shouldn't go wandering about mountainsides on your own," observed Crispin. "If you had tripped on the path which leads up the Schwarzberg, your accident could have been serious. You might even have stumbled over the edge of the cliffs, and then," he added sardonically, "it would take a lot more than a small cognac to pull you together again!"

His words were so near the mark, they sent a

shiver down my spine as I raised my glass to my lips, and the amber liquid slopped over the brim.

"Whatever is the matter?" asked Niall sharply.

"A goose over my grave!" I tried to laugh the shiver away.

"Or a too vivid imagination?" Jon Crispin's eyes were mocking.

"You sound as if you were the one with the vivid imagination!" I retorted sharply, giving him a cold look.

"How right you are." The mockery changed to amusement. "If I did not have imagination in my profession I would starve!"

Niall looked at him with interest. "You live by your imagination? You must be a writer." He frowned. "Crispin," he repeated the other man's name. "Jon Crispin, of course! I wondered where I had heard your name before. You must be the fellow who writes the spy thrillers!"

Before Crispin could acknowledge the fact, there was a disturbance in the hall outside. An excited voice called:

"Herr Katz! Herr Katz!"

Next moment, Hans Schmidt, the simple old woodcutter and odd job man who helped about the Gasthof, came into the parlour.

"Wo ist Herr Katz?" he demanded.

His eyes were staring wildly, his whole body shook as if with ague, and saliva trickled from the corners of his trembling mouth.

"What is wrong, old man?" The barman hurried from behind the counter and made Hans sit down in a chair.

"What is wrong, Hans?" he repeated. "Don't you feel well?"

The old man gaped up at him. "There has been another terrible accident, Heinrich!" he babbled shakily. "Rudi is lying all smashed up near our little shrine." He crossed himself. "I think—I think—I think—" His voice trembled so much he had difficulty in forming his sentence, and he could not get beyond the first words.

Niall climbed down from the bar stool and went over to the old man.

"Steady, old fellow. Take it slowly and tell us what has happened."

His calmness had the desired effect. Hans seemed to pull himself together.

"Rudi must have fallen over the mountain," he spoke quite clearly. "He is lying under the spot where the escarpment overhangs. Where we had all the landslides last winter."

Niall looked across at the barman.

"I think you had better telephone for a doctor and an ambulance, and see if you can get hold of Herr Katz.

"Crispin, in the meantime, I think you and I should rig up a stretcher of sorts and see if we can bring the accident victim back here. I know something of first aid."

Old Hans shook his head. "You would be better with the priest than the doctor. Rudi is dying. How he lived so long after a fall like that, I cannot understand."

"You mean to say he is still alive?" gasped Heinrich.

"Jah!" the old man nodded, "but I do not think he will last long."

"In that case, the sooner we get to him the better," said Niall briskly. "Miranda, go and see if Liesl has a first aid kit, and Crispin, you go and get some blankets. I know where I can lay my hands on a couple of poles," but Crispin wasn't there to obey his order.

He had grabbed old Hans and was urging him out of the room to lead the way to the dying man, and while Niall, whose command of the situation I had admired, went dashing after them, I sat on, shocked to inaction, unwarmed by the brandy I had hastily gulped back when Hans had blurted out his tragic news.

There could be no doubt that the man the old woodcutter had found dying was the same Rudi who had been pushed to his death, in my hearing, up there on the Schwarzberg.

What was more, I happened to have my eyes on Jon Crispin when the old man had been speaking, and there had been an odd gleam in his eye when Hans announced that Rudi was still alive.

Was it mere ghoulish interest to be in on an event which would make first-rate material for one of his thrillers, or had there been something more personal involved, in the way he had gone dashing out from the bar with Hans, without attending to Niall's commands, and without even taking a second to swallow the last mouthful of beer?

Was I reading too much into his actions? Was

I supersensitive after my ordeal on the Schwarz-berg?

All I knew was that if I had been scared up there on the Alpine mountainside, I was even more scared now, as I sat perched on the bar stool of the Schwarzberghof.

For the first time, I was appreciating that the men who had killed Rudi might be men I knew, even if only casually, and I wished with all my heart that I could be anywhere else in the world but where I was!

Chapter Three

An ashen-faced Liesl came rushing into the bar as I was getting off the stool to go in search of her.

"Miranda! Heinrich tells me there has been an accident! Who was hurt? Are the injuries bad?"

"Very bad," I said gravely. "It seems that some man called Rudi slipped from the path on the Schwarzberg. Hans found him lying near the little shrine."

"Oh, no!" Liesl let out a shuddering sigh. "Not another accident! Will there never be an end to them?" she cried. "Nothing, but nothing seems to have gone right since dear Papa died!" She ran weeping from the room.

"Liesl!" I hurried after her. "What is the matter with you?"

She stopped and dabbed her eyes with her apron.

"Come up to your room, Miranda. We can talk there."

She led the way upstairs, and once we were in my bedroom, she surprised me by locking the door behind her.

In a whisper, almost as if she were afraid of being overheard, she told me to sit down, and then she began her tale of woe.

"I do not exaggerate, Miranda, when I tell you this place has never been the same since Papa died.

"First one thing, then another, seemed to go wrong. There were avalanches and rock falls on the mountain, which buried one of our best high pasture lands. Then Mama went and married this man Katz!" She almost spat out her stepfather's name.

"How I hate that man!" she spoke passionately. "He has brought ill luck. The cowmen who used to work for us did not like his bossy ways and left. We have difficulty keeping staff in the Gasthof because of his high-handed manners. Truly, Miranda, this husband of my mother's has brought nothing but bad luck with him to our home."

"Don't be silly, Liesl!" I protested. "You are still unhappy from your father's death. You and he were so close. For the time being you are only seeing the black side of things."

"Why did my mother have to marry again so soon?" wailed Liesl. "It was only weeks after he was buried that Katz came to visit us. It seems he was a friend of Mama's in Munich, when she was a girl."

"He sounds as if he was one of her former admirers," I admitted. "Possibly one she spurned in favour of your father."

"She didn't have to marry him," said Liesl sullenly.

"Perhaps she was glad to have a man help her with the farm and the guest-house. It is not easy for a woman on her own to cope with a place like this."

"She had Joseph and I!"

"She might even have felt the need of a man's guidance where you were concerned."

"That's rubbish! I am of age and old enough to help with family problems. If it had been someone else, it might not have been so bad—but this man! Miranda! I do not like him! No one does!"

"That's silly. Obviously your mother does, or she would not have married him."

"Please, Miranda, listen to me! I tell you others feel about him as I do—even the guests who were in the habit of coming to the Inn, year after year after year have not come back this summer! Some, I know for a fact, have returned to other guest-houses in the district, so it is not because they grew tired of the locality they did not come here. No!" she said stormily, "it is because of my step-father. He does not make our guests welcome, as father used to.

"He is aloof from them. There is no more singing in the bar parlour in the evening. No more communal gaiety. It is as if the life had gone from the place."

She stopped, rose from the bed on which she had been sitting during her tirade, tiptoed to the door and peeped out as if she suspected that someone in the corridor had been listening to her words. She closed the door softly once more, and stood with her back to it.

"I do not want to be disloyal, Miranda, but I must talk to someone. Herr Katz—I can never think of him as one of the family—is so domineering he makes me hate him!

"He likes things to be done just so. We must

all live to a timetable, so that he knows where we are, and what we are doing, each minute of the day. It is like being back at school, or in the Army!"

"Poor Liesl!" I shook my head in sympathy. "You do have it in for your step-father, don't you? But don't you think you are exaggerating just a little?" I suggested.

"Herr Katz probably finds your own easy-going approach to life as irritating as you find his adherence to routine. Moreover," I paused, hesitating before my next words, "don't you honestly think there could be some of the green-eyed monster in your attitude to your mother's husband? I mean, it would be only natural for you to feel subconscious resentment at this stranger for taking your own father's place in the home."

Liesl sighed, and moved across to sit once more on the edge of the bed.

"That is exactly how Franz explains it! When I tell him I find Herr Katz is cold and harsh and somewhat frightening, he tells me I am looking for faults where none exist, because I am jealous of my mother's love for her new husband. He says that while Katz is not so jovial and such good company as my papa was, he is not a bad sort."

"Franz always was a level-headed young man," I said, in full agreement with his sentiments.

Then I shot Liesl a quizzical look. "I am surprised that you and Franz haven't got married yet. I felt sure that when I came to Schwartzberg this summer, you would be Mrs. Franz Grillparzer!"

Liesl blushed. "Surely, you know you would have been asked as a guest to my wedding, Miranda! As it is, I hope you will return to Schwarzberg in the autumn, for that is when we have set the date for our marriage."

"Liesl!" I exclaimed joyfully. "I am so glad!" I rose from my seat and embraced her warmly.

"Once you are married, you can forget about your step-father and your dislike of him, and settle happily in your own home.

"Why!" I went on, "you may even learn to be in sympathy with him! After all," I pointed out, "it could not have been easy for the poor man to take on the responsibility of two grown-up children." I smiled. "What does your brother think of him, by the way?"

"That is what I find most surprising!" exclaimed Liesl. "Joseph thinks the world of his new father. He follows him around everywhere, and copies his mannerisms. Hadn't you noticed?"

"I have only been here a couple of days," I protested. "I haven't noticed anything unusual in Joseph's behaviour."

As I spoke, I wondered if Liesl's brother's affection for his step-father might be another reason for my friend's dislike of the man. On my previous visits to the Schwarzberghof, it had often irritated me the way young Joseph trailed around after his sister and me.

Liesl stood up. "I tell you what, Miranda," she said, with a return to her natural cheerfulness, "I shall make some coffee, and we shall have our 'Jause' up here in your bedroom, and I shall tell you about Franz's new job in Salzburg, and our plans for our new home.

"We have not had a chance for a real talk together since you came. Either Herr Katz has seen to it that I am kept busy in the kitchen, or tending the prize cows in the byre, or that tall, fair, nice-looking Englishman, Paterson, has been monopolizing your attention!" She dimpled. "I think you have made a conquest there!"

She bustled from the room, and I went to sit down on the hand-carved, wooden rocking chair by the window, to look out over the meadows which sloped steeply down to the lower belt of pine woods, whose lofty branches hid the little hamlet of Schwarzberg from view of the guesthouse.

The only hint that habitations lay beyond that deep green sea of treetops was the thin spire and the golden, onion-shaped dome of the village church, which seemed to sprout like an outsize fruit of paradise from the trees which concealed the rest of the building.

It was six, no, seven summers ago, since I had first come to this part of Austria.

I had been studying German at school, and Liesl Langheim's name had been given to me as my German pen friend. We had corresponded diligently for three years, and then Liesl had invited me to her home in Schwarzberg for the first month of my summer vacation.

Up to that time, I had never travelled abroad, and I was almost sick with excitement at the invitation. My parents flew with me to Paris, and waved me to a rather tearful farewell at the Gare de L'Est as I boarded the Arlberg-Orient Express. Through the window of the compartment, they warned me over and over again about making friends with strangers. This struck me as funny, for was I not on my way to stay with people none of us had ever met?

By the time the night-express pulled out of the station, scurried through the spasmodically lit suburbs of the French capital, and plunged into the darkness of the countryside on its way to Belfort, I had dried my tears and was all agog with the adventure ahead.

I couldn't relax. I sat on the edge of my seat from Paris to Belfort, from Belfort to the excitement of the crossing of the frontier to Switzerland at Bâle, and as the express hurtled through the night, I made no effort to sleep but sat rigidly staring out of the window, seeing nothing there but my own big-eyed, pale-cheeked reflection.

I was still awake, on that first journey, as we left Switzerland for Austria, but my eyes felt sore and strained as I peered out at the towering hills in the first light of dawn, and read the magic names, Feldkirch, St. Anton, and so on until at long last, shortly after mid-day, the express stopped at Innsbruck's main station.

Cramped and weary, I grasped my luggage and descended to the platform. Almost before my feet touched the ground, I was warmly greeted by a small, round, cheerful-faced man with a Tyrolean hat perched gaily on his thinning locks.

"Miranda!" he embraced me warmly without self-consciousness. "I recognized you at once from your photographs! Welcome to Austria!"

He took my cases from me, while his daughter, Liesl, plump, pretty and smiling, greeted me shyly.

I have never forgotten that first moment. Herr Langheim made me feel at home from the word go. He chatted amiably as he led me from the station to a restaurant in nearby Maria Theresienstrasse, where he told Liesl to take me to the ladies' room to wash myself and freshen up after my long journey, and by the time I returned to the dining-room, he had ordered an enormous meal, "to help fill up the hollows of my face" as he put it, and not until he was satisfied I had had enough to eat did he lead me back along the famous street to where he had parked his car.

Liesl and I, our initial shyness past, chattered like magpies in a mixture of English and German, while Herr Langheim drove us to his home, a guest-house some forty miles from Innsbruck, high up among the mountains of the Tyrol.

From that first day, Liesl and I were firm friends. Her father was like a favourite uncle, her small brother, Joseph, was an amiable nuisance, like all small brothers, and her attractive-looking mother, although a shade more austere and reserved than her jolly husband, always treated me with great kindness.

I loved being with them, and it was not only

the Langheim family which enchanted me. I loved their chalet-type guest-house, which was also a farm with byres attached to the back of the main building. I loved the surrounding meadows and the high, mysterious looking mountain, the Schwarzberg, which gave its name to the village which nestled at its foot.

Liesl showed me all her favourite haunts and taught me how to climb the mountains, and told me the local folk lore, so that that first summer, and in the summers to come, I learned to know the Schwarzberg and its neighbourhood, Innsbruck, Telfs, and all the villages between, as well as Liesl learned to know about my home in Angus and the surrounding country, when she came to stay with me. For after that first visit of mine to Austria, Liesl returned home with me for a month, and this set the pattern for our holidays for the next five years.

I would spend a month with Leisl in Austria and she would return to spend a month with me in Scotland. I learned to speak German fluently, but with the local accent of Schwarzberg. Liesl's English had a distinctively Scottish flavour!

Last year, the pattern had been altered because of Liesl's father's death and my own mother's illness; but I had been determined to come back to Schwarzberg this year on my way home from Graz University, where I had been doing a course after graduating at St. Andrews.

At first, I had been delighted to return, even if it had been strange to find that Liesl's mother had married again, and to be welcomed by a tall, fair haired, burly, stern-faced host instead of by my dear stout, cheerful 'Uncle' Langheim.

As I gazed reminiscently out of the window, away to the right I could see the rock face above the spot where I had been sunbathing that afternoon, and as I looked I was reminded sharply of the murder I had heard being committed, and of the poor man who had been pushed to a pain-filled death.

I shivered. Between Liesl's dislike of her step-father, the more formal atmosphere I sensed at the Gasthof, and the afternoon's ordeal, I began to wish I had not tried to pick up the threads of the old holiday pattern.

With a jerk, I pushed the rocking chair back from the window and stood up. This would definitely be my last visit to Schwarzberg, I decided. When Liesl married, and went to live in Salzburg, no one could expect me to return, and so I need never again see the grim mountain which would always remind me that I had let selfishness interfere with conscience in failing to report what I knew of Rudi's death, and so let two villains get away with murder.

As I thought these gloomy thoughts, Liesl came back to the bedroom, but she was not carrying the promised tray of cakes and coffee.

"The ambulance has arrived, Miranda, and two policemen—one of them an Inspector! They are waiting out in the yard for Mr. Paterson and the others to bring the climber back." She slammed the bedroom door angrily.

"Why can't people act sensibly on the mountains!" she raged. "Why do they do careless things, which bring disaster on themselves and involve others in their foolishness!"

"You seem to have quite a number of accidents in the area, the way you speak," I said in surprise. "I can't say I ever remember any taking place all the times I was here before."

"That was because you always came at the quiet season for tourists." Liesl paced the floor restlessly. "At the height of the summer, when the place is full of visitors, there are often mishaps.

"It makes me so angry, Miranda! So many of these incidents could be avoided, if people only used their commonsense. Do you know," she shook her head, "some of the people who come here do not seem to realize that going for a walk in the mountains is any different from going for a stroll in a city park!

"These Dummköpfe wander from the inns and hotels without thinking of telling anyone where they propose to go. The pleasant sunlight, the soft, pine-needle carpeted pathways through the trees, tempt them to walk on and on. They climb higher up the mountains than they are aware of doing. They scramble off the main track looking for Alpine flowers or better views of the valley beneath them. Then they lose their way! They wear shoes with thin slippery soles which were never intended to keep a foothold on rough and dangerous mountain terrain. They wear sleeveless shirts, and shorts, and summer dresses, because it is warm in the valley from which they set off, never realizing that a few hundred feet higher up such clothes will be no protection against the ice-cold winds which can come blustering down without warning, from the snow-covered ridges of the Wetterstein Gebirge, and they forget, too, that there are such things as low cloud and sudden, swirling mountain mists.

"They get into all sorts of difficulties, these foolish city climbers, and then the locals, however busy they are, however dangerous the job, must go out and rescue them.

"The lucky ones are quickly found, suffering perhaps only from exposure and fright. The unluckier ones are often ill for months from broken limbs and prolonged exposure to cold and damp.

"The luckless ones," Liesl's expressive eyes shrouded in pity, "like this poor man Hans found today, go plunging to their deaths from faulty footholds, following over-confidence in their climbing abilities!"

Chapter Four

A clatter of footsteps from the cobbled yard under the small side window of my bedroom broke the long silence which followed Liesl's bitter speech about amateur hill climbers.

I crossed to the small aperture and looked out.

Herr Katz and Johan Werner, one of the guests in the Gasthof, were walking across the yard towards one of the big cattle sheds which adjoined the back of the main building. They were carrying a make-shift stretcher on which lay a blanket-covered heap.

Behind them, wordless as a funeral procession, followed Hans, the old man who had found the body, his eyes staring straight ahead of him, his lips moving silently as if in prayer, and then Jon Crispin and Niall Paterson walking side by side, and bringing up the rear the tall, lovely blonde girl who was married to Johan Werner.

Crispin and Niall looked grim, but Irma Werner's face was expressionless.

"Your step-father and Werner have saved the ambulance men a walk," I informed Liesl, who had made no move to follow me to the window. "They have brought the man here."

"Is he still alive?" she whispered hopefully.

I shook my head.

"Oh! Why do such things happen when Mama is away!" she exclaimed bitterly. "Accidents like this upset me so! My step-father can't understand it—he says I am far too soft."

There was a knock on the door and Joseph, Liesl's young brother, called:

"Liesl! Are you there? Father wants you to come down and make coffee for everyone. You had better hurry!"

"Coming!" called Liesl, then she turned to me and said in an angry whisper, "You see what I mean? I am expected to be on call to help at all times! And Joseph has grown so bossy! Did you hear the cheeky way he spoke to me?"

"Liesl, don't upset yourself. I shall come down with you and give you a hand."

"You must not do that!" said Liesl, unlocking the door and leading the way downstairs. "My step-father would disapprove."

"Nonsense!" I said firmly. "He needn't know. He will be too busy in the yard to know what is going on in the kitchen."

"Joseph would be sure to tell him," she sighed. "I can manage all right on my own, thanks, Miranda."

She went to the kitchen and I hovered at the front door, wanting to know what had happened, yet not liking to go out and ask.

Niall Paterson, who was talking to one of the police officers in remarkably fluent German, noticed me and signalled me back into the house.

"I shall join you shortly," he called.

I went back into the cool shadows of the Gasthof, and along the narrow, stone-flagged passage which led from the door out to the yard to the living-room.

This was a long, low-ceilinged apartment, with two wide, double-glazed windows which overlooked the square of orchard in front of the house, an orchard which served the double purpose of providing fruits for jams and jellies and preserves in summer, and of acting as a kind of windbreak in the cold, blustery winter days.

One of the pear trees in the orchard, which Uncle Langheim had told me was as old as the house itself, was so high that its topmost branch overhung the roof at the gable end of the house, and lower branches brushed against the wide window of my bedroom.

Like the bar parlour, the living-room of the Gasthof was panelled in a very dark wood, with ornately carved stags' heads holding up the mantelshelf over the fireplace.

A couple of old-fashioned paintings, the equivalent, I imagined, of our "Stag at Bay" type of illustration, adorned the far wall, and in the four corners of the room were large pots, like black witches' cauldrons, from which grew smooth-leaved rubber plants and ivies which were trained up the walls and along the top ledges of the panelling.

The effect of these furnishings would have been depressing if the dark tones of the wood and the ivies had not been relieved by the plump, velvet, scarlet-coloured cushions on the armchairs and along the window seats; and an enormous glazed jug full of every colourful mountain flower of the region, which was set out on the long, low table which stood to one side of the smouldering pine wood fire.

I sat down on the couch and stared glumly at the almost dead embers in the grate. Was I doing the right thing, I wondered, in continuing to say nothing to anyone about my experience on the Schwarzberg?

"A couple of these logs will soon bring that dismal fire to life!"

Jon Crispin's voice behind me made me turn round with a violent start.

He was taken aback by my startled reaction.

"I am sorry, Miss MacIntosh! I did not mean to frighten you," he said, as he flung a couple of logs on the ashes and brushed the resin, which had oozed from the pine wood, from his hands.

"You must be very much on edge," he eyed me keenly.

"I didn't hear you come into the room," I said shortly.

"Your mind must have been miles away if you didn't hear that door creak when I opened it!" he observed. "You look upset about something. Can I help?"

I frowned, annoyed at his perspicacity.

"I am not worried about anything," I denied quickly.

"No?" Crispin kicked the logs he had placed on the fire into sparkling life.

"I could have sworn you were." He paused. "You didn't happen to know this man Rudi who was killed, did you?" he probed. "There was something in the way you acted when old Hans broke his news, which made me think you might."

I controlled a guilty start with a mighty effort of will.

"What nonsense!" I said tartly. "If I had

known the man, I would have been the first to go to see if I could be of help to him. No, Mr. Crispin," I denied. "I did not know this Rudi person. I am afraid your novelist's imagination has been running away with you!" I sneered.

Crispin shook his head.

"The old man's announcement definitely affected you."

"Naturally!" I responded. "I hate hearing of tragic accidents, especially so near to home. 'No man is an island.' I expect you know the rest of that passage from John Donne's famous sermon."

Jon Crispin turned from the fire and stared down at me.

"Indeed, I do, Miss MacIntosh." He capped the quotation, " 'Any man's death diminishes me, because I am involved in mankind.' " He continued to study my face, and his direct look made me feel uncomfortable.

"I still think, Miss MacIntosh, that—"

But whatever Crispin thought, I was destined not to hear, because our uncomfortable, for me, tête-à-tête was interrupted by the arrival of Niall Paterson, and I let out a faint sigh of relief at his opportune entry into the room.

Niall was followed by the two police officials, and, seconds later, Irma and Johan Werner appeared with Herr Katz and old Hans, the woodcutter, following close behind.

Poor old Hans was in a shocked state. He did not seem fully aware of his surroundings as he skulked behind Katz's back, his rheumy eyes dull and his slack old mouth forming soundless words.

Katz asked everyone to sit down. The Werners sat together under one of the pictures. Niall came over beside me. The police officials sat on the window seat, their backs to the light, while Katz and old Hans remained standing near the doorway. Crispin stood lounging against the fireplace, his keen gaze sweeping round the room.

There was an uneasy silence in the room while everyone settled themselves, a silence which was fortunately quickly interrupted by the arrival of Liesl, carrying a tray load of coffee cups and a heavy percolator.

Jon Crispin straightened up and moved quickly across the floor to relieve my friend of her load and carry it to the long low table beside me. I removed the jug of flowers to give him room to set it down, and Liesl who had stopped, momentarily taken aback, I think, by Crispin's helpfulness, stepped towards us.

As she did so, old Hans, who had known Liesl since she was a babe in arms, clutched at her arm with his rheumatism-gnarled fingers and halted her progress.

He peered at her, anxious eyed, his trembling mouth continuing to form soundless words, as if shock and excitement had combined to deprive him of his power of speech. Liesl gently removed his hand from her arm.

"There, there, Hans. Don't upset yourself," she said kindly. "The police aren't going to harm you."

Hans caught at her arm again, and this time his whole body seemed to shake in his effort to force his vocal chords into action.

The others in the room looked away in embarrassment. I stood up to pour the coffee for Liesl, and one of the policemen started to speak.

"I cannot understand," he said, his eyes roving the room from one face to the next, "how Rudi Schneider came to trip over the cliff. He was the most reliable and experienced mountain guide in the region."

"It takes only a second of inattention to precipitate disaster," observed Niall. He sounded rather pompous, as if on his best court-room behaviour.

"That is the point," stressed the official. "I have never known Rudi to be careless on the mountains. He knew only too well what the cost could be. He had taken part in too many rescues of thoughtless mountaineers ever to forget the lessons taught by such accidents. Moreover," he frowned, "I have climbed up this particular path on the Schwarzberg myself many times. Apart from the fact that the track runs along the edge of the cliff face, it is not particularly difficult and it is fairly broad. A man of Rudi's experience would not have walked close to the outside of the path for fear of part of it crumbling away. No," he repeated, "I cannot understand how the accident—" was it my imagination, or did he accent the word?—"happened."

"You sound as if you don't think it *was* an accident." The words were out of my mouth before I could stop them.

When I finished speaking, every eye in the room switched to my face, and I could feel my cheeks crimson.

"My dear Miranda!" Niall's voice pitied me. "What else could it have been?"

I lowered my lashes so that he could not read my thoughts. The word "murder" hovered on my tongue, yet still I was afraid to utter it.

"Perhaps Miss MacIntosh thinks the man may have deliberately thrown himself over the edge?" It was Johan Werner who posed me this question.

I licked my lips nervously.

"I think Miss MacIntosh is sentimental, like all her race." Irma Werner's interruption saved me from replying. "She perhaps thinks this man had an unhappy love affair, and rather than face life without the woman he loved," she sneered, "he committed suicide."

At her words, old Hans pulled himself away from Liesl and crossed himself.

"Suicide!" he screeched at Irma in a high falsetto. "This was never suicide!"

Having recovered his ability to speak, he was determined not to lose it, and he babbled on,

"Rudi Schneider was a good Catholic. He would never have taken his own life! But perhaps," he peered at the elegant blonde with sly eyes, "that is what you would like people to think, hein?

"Suicide! Or a careless accident!" He shook his head from side to side. "Oh, no! You can't fool me." His weak eyes watered as he peered round the room, looking at each face in turn. "Young Rudi's death was neither, do you hear me?" His voice rose hysterically. "Oh, no! It was neither suicide, nor yet an accident!"

He gasped for breath and clutched at his throat as though so many words, spoken in such excitement, had caused it to ache.

The taller of the two police officials stood up and crossed over to stand looking down at the shaky old wood-cutter.

"What are you driving at, old man?" he demanded sternly.

Hans looked up at him defiantly.

"Rudi was pushed over the cliff!"

There was a concerted gasp from everyone present.

The policeman grabbed Hans' arm.

"Be careful what you say, Schmidt!"

"Rudi was pushed!" squawked the old man for a second time. "He told me so himself, when I found him!"

If anyone had struck a match, I felt sure the room would have blown up, so explosive was the air.

"Yes," gabbled Hans. "Poor Rudi was very near death's door when I found him, but by God's will he lived long enough to let me know the truth of how he came to be lying there.

"When he saw me bending over him, he whispered these very words, 'Hans! They pushed me!' He said the same thing twice, as if to make sure I understood, and do you know?—" Old Hans wrinkled his brow in a puzzled frown. "Come to think of it—Rudi sounded very surprised! Almost as if whoever had sent him over the ledge had been someone he knew and trusted!"

Chapter Five

Herr Katz was the first to break the startled silence which followed Hans' statement.

"Hans! Pull yourself together, Dummköpf!" His voice was stern. "You are babbling a lot of nonsense. There is not a soul in this community who would do Rudi Schneider harm," he scoffed. "Too many of us owe him either our own lives, or the lives of our friends."

Hans stared sullenly at his master, and repeated stubbornly, "I know what Rudi said. I was there, wasn't I?"

"I shouldn't pay any attention to the old man, Inspector Bauer," Katz spoke as if Hans was not present. "He has always been simple minded, you know."

"And I daresay the shock of finding the body has thrown him right off balance." Johan Werner looked at the old wood-cutter with pitying eyes.

"I don't think Schneider was even alive when Hans found him, far less able to speak coherently," put in Irma Werner.

"You see," she explained, "Johan and I were walking along the side of the meadow, not very far behind Hans when he made his discovery." She twisted her broad golden wedding ring round and round her finger as she talked.

"We saw him bend down over what we thought from the distance was a bundle of rags, but it wasn't minutes before he straightened up and started to run towards the Gasthof. He seemed so excited we called after him to find out if there was anything wrong, but he did not seem to hear us.

"Our curiosity was aroused, so that we left the path and made our way to the bundle. When we realized it was a man lying there, Johan knelt down to see how badly he was injured, but the man was dead."

I looked across the room at Irma.

She recounted her story impersonally, as if the afternoon tragedy had merely been an annoying incident which had spoilt her enjoyment of the afternoon; an annoying incident, and nothing more. She appeared quite unmoved by the fact that a man had died so tragically.

"You were not there! I did not see you!" Hans' voice shrilled into my thoughts. "You are lying!"

"That will be enough, Hans," said Katz angrily. "You have insulted my guests. Leave this room at once! I can forgive you many things because of your age and simplicity, but this behaviour I will not tolerate."

"A moment, please."

The official I had heard referred to as Inspector Bauer stepped forward and laid a detaining arm on Hans' arm.

"Old man, you are the one who first reported finding the body, jah?"

Hans nodded.

"Then, tell me this. It was lying off the track. How did you spot it? Did you see it fall from the cliff?"

The old man peered slyly up into the Inspector's face.

"I have told you all I know. If you do not care to believe me, because I am old Hans, and I do not tell the same story as a posh lady and gentleman from Germany, that is your affair." He clawed away the detaining hand, and turned to leave the room.

"That is no way to talk to Inspector Bauer!" Katz pulled him back. "Apologize to him for your rudeness."

"Hans did not mean to be impolite." Heinrich the barman interceded for the old man.

"He is not quite himself. Sometimes he imagines things, and he could not have seen Mr. and Mrs. Werner, because he has cataract in both eyes and can only see objects clearly at close range."

"That would explain why he did not notice us," nodded Herr Werner.

"He doesn't happen to be deaf, too, does he?" Jon Crispin eyed the barman sardonically, and Hans shrank back from the stare of the disbelieving eyes around him, and he began to mutter away to himself again in confusion. Tears welled from his weak old eyes and ran down the deep wrinkles of his weather-beaten face.

"For pity's sake!" I cried angrily. "Can't you leave the old soul alone? Haven't you the sense to see that the more you badger him, the less coherent he will become?"

Impulsively I went over to the old man and put my arm gently around him.

"Come, Hans," I said, ignoring the surprise on

the faces of the police and his other inquisitors, "Liesl and I will take care of you. We believe you," and heedless of a protest from Katz, I led the trembling woodman from the room, along to the kitchen with Liesl following close behind.

No one made any effort to stop us, and I was glad, because by the time I reached the kitchen and settled Hans on a bench near the stove, my legs were so shaky I had to sit down myself.

"Miranda! You were wonderful!" breathed Liesl goggle-eyed. "The way you took charge of Hans, and swept the police protestations aside! I could never have done anything like that."

"I was angry," I told her. "I hate seeing anyone browbeaten."

"My step-father was the worst!" said Liesl. "I think he would like an excuse to get rid of Hans."

"I think he was chiefly annoyed at the way Hans spoke to Frau Werner," I replied. "As innkeeper, he could hardly be expected to condone the way Hans miscalled her, although I do agree he was over-harsh."

Liesl prepared fresh coffee, and gave me a cup to give to Hans. I added some cognac to the brew, and the old man eagerly gulped it down, although it didn't seem to do much to stop the shivering in his limbs.

"Do you think we should try to put him to bed, Liesl?" I asked softly. "My opinion is that he has had as much as he can take for one day, poor old soul."

"So you do involve yourself in mankind, Miss MacIntosh. You weren't using words merely for

effect?" For the second time that afternoon Jon
Crispin's voice made me turn round with a start.
He advanced into the room, looking at me cu-
riously.

"You rather took the wind out of everyone's
sails the way you flew to the defence of old
Hans," he continued. "I don't think Inspector
Bauer was very pleased, the way you whipped
him away from the interrogation chamber!"

"I don't give a damn whether the Inspector
was pleased or not!" I said tartly. "I wasn't
going to stand there doing nothing while Hans
was being reduced to a gibbering nonentity. A
man in the Inspector's position should know the
truth when he hears it, and not go on bullying
an old man until he gets all muddled up with his
story."

Crispin's thick black eyebrows shot up. "You
believe what the old man said, don't you?"

"Hans isn't a novelist!" I retorted, looking
steadily into Crispin's hazel eyes. "He would not
have the kind of imagination you have to con-
coct such an improbable tale."

"I don't suppose he would." Crispin looked
down at the old man's grizzled head, as he sat on
the bench nodding to himself.

"I wonder if Rudi said anything else to him?
If he named any names?"

His words seemed to penetrate the old man's
mind, because he looked up and mumbled something, but his words were slurred and indistin-
guishable.

"I think you gave him too much brandy,
Miranda," Liesl said in a worried tone. "Look at

him! He looks as if he is going to fall asleep on the bench, and we can't let him do that. Herr Katz would be furious!"

"Tell me where he lives, and I'll take him there." Jon Crispin stooped down and lifted the frail old man up in his arms, as if he were a child.

"He has a room behind the cow shed," said Liesl. "Come, I shall show you."

She led the way from the kitchen out into the yard, past the byres where the cattle brought in from the meadow were lowing contentedly in stalls, which were as immaculate as could be and sweetly scented with fresh hay.

The byres were actually attached to the rear of the Gasthof, giving the building the shape of a capital L. Behind the byres, a compartment which had once been a stable had been converted into a small dwelling, which was the woodcutter's home. There was still a through door connecting stable and byre, because prior to Hans being given the apartment, it had been the home of the byreman, and it had suited this man to have direct access to the byres.

The walls of the room were whitewashed, and the thick stone slabbing of the floor was covered with straw mats. A table and a couple of easy chairs, not unlike the ones in the living-room of the Gasthof itself, were drawn up in one corner, and at the other side of the room was an old-fashioned wardrobe, a heavy wooden chest and a narrow truckle bed covered with a "plumeau".

The only ornament in the room was a crucifix on the bare wall opposite the window, and below the crucifix, on a small plant table, was a jam jar filled with meadow flowers and a framed photograph of the old man's wife and sons.

A paraffin stove in the middle of the room was burning low. It was of the type which could not be easily upset, I noticed, as I turned up the flame.

Liesl turned back the plumeau, and Jon Crispin gently deposited the already sleeping woodcutter on the bed, where he expertly managed to divest him of his shoes and outer wear without disturbing him, and then covered him with the soft down quilt.

"He should sleep till morning." Jon looked down at the sleeping figure. "Poor old man!" he observed softly as he turned away.

Liesl glanced at her watch. "Oh, dear! I hadn't realized how late it was. I shall have to hurry and peel the potatoes for the evening meal!"

She pursed her lips. "I wonder if Inspector Bauer and the other man will be staying on?"

"I heard them say they would be leaving shortly," said Crispin, "and for that matter, the Werners told me earlier in the day that they are going to Exl Bühne in Innsbruck tonight, so that will be two less for you to provide for."

"Oh, good!" said Liesl. "I hate doing the catering when Mama is away. I cannot think of enough variety for the menus, and Mrs. Werner looks as if she was accustomed to a cordon bleu cuisine!"

Chapter Six

Liesl hurried off to her kitchen and I was left on my own with Jon Crispin.

I felt ill at ease. This whole day had been a strange one, from my frightening ordeal on the Schwarzberg to my meeting with this disconcerting stranger, Jon Crispin; from the announcement of old Hans that he had found the body of the man whose death scream I had heard to the present moment when I had helped the old wood-cutter to his bed.

Like old Hans, I felt that I had had as much as I could take, and the thought of going back to the Gasthof and making conversation with a lot of strangers did not appeal. It seemed a part of my present run of luck that Liesl's mother should be away from home, so that my friend was too busy taking over from her mother to have time for me.

If Liesl's father had been alive, I could have turned to him for advice and comfort, and as I thought of him, I couldn't help agreeing with Liesl that with her father's death the luck of the Schwarzberghof had changed.

I began to wish I had never thought of stopping off here for a holiday on my way home. The whole atmosphere of the place was different from the old days.

If I had the imaginative powers of the man who was standing beside me, I would probably have said that with the death of its former jovial host, joy had gone from the Gasthof.

"A penny for them?" Jon Crispin's voice broke into my self-pitying thoughts.

I knocked away a horse fly which had been clinging, unnoticed, on my hand until it had drawn blood.

"I think I shall move on from here tomorrow," I said. "I came for relaxation, and the enjoyment of Liesl's company, after a hard term's work." I pouted. "Today's goings on are not conducive to relaxation, and with Liesl's mother away on holiday it seems there will be little time for us to get together."

"There certainly is not much for a young woman to do in an isolated spot like this," agreed Crispin. "I am not surprised you want to get away."

"I used to love being here," I spoke half to myself. "In the old days, there always seemed to be plenty of ways to amuse myself, and never enough time to do half of the things I wanted to do."

Thinking of the past, I walked idly across the yard and through the orchard to the narrow track which served as a short cut across the meadows, through the lower belt of pine trees, to the village of Schwarzberg.

Crispin fell into step beside me.

"I gather you have spent a previous holiday here?"

"Liesl and I have been friends for years," I explained, and I found myself telling him how our friendship had come about, and about the happy holidays we had spent over the years in each other's homes.

"When I couldn't come here last year, the year Herr Langheim, Liesl's father, died, because of my own mother's illness, I determined I must make an effort to see her this year."

I plucked a piece of long grass from the field through which we were passing.

"But even without taking into account what happened today, nothing seems to be the same. Perhaps it is because Liesl's father is dead, and he was part of the fun and magic Schwarzberghof used to hold for me. Herr Langheim was a poppet! Always laughing, always thinking of things for us to do; always bringing a zest to whatever we did.

"Liesl is very like him in appearance—small and dark and plump. He never walked where he could swagger—if you know what I mean.

"At night there would be sing-songs in the bar parlour. Everyone would join in! Often Uncle Langheim and his friends would perform one of those clapping Tyrolean dances. It was great fun!

"During the day we would help with the cattle or the haymaking, or we would spend the whole day long climbing and exploring the mountainside, hoping to find a secret way through the landslides to Rohrdorf Castle." I smiled.

"We never did, of course! But it was fun to pretend that we might.

"Then, if we tired of exploring and helping with the farm work, we would talk the summer visitors into taking us to Innsbruck as guides, and after we had shown them the sights of the town, we would go to the Alt Insprugg for coffee and cakes—" I sighed wistfully. "It was all wonderful!"

"It couldn't have gone on for ever." Jon Crispin sat down on an old tree trunk and I sat down, hugging my knees, on a soft cushion of pine needles.

"Even if Herr Langheim hadn't died, things would have changed," he said. "Those things you enjoyed doing as a schoolgirl, you couldn't keep on doing now. You are an adult now, my dear. Young women of your age can't go exploring mountains, looking for dream castles!"

"Rohrdorf Castle isn't a dream castle," I assured him. "It exists all right. And it has quite a history! It was built as a hunting lodge for some Bavarian princeling. Later it came into the hands of General Freistadt of the S.S.—I expect you have heard of his reputation!"

"Who hasn't?" said Crispin grimly.

"During the war, it was put to use as a convalescent home for German airmen, and then, at the end of the war, it was one of the last Nazi strongholds this side of the border.

"Up until 1945 there was a road of sorts through the Schwarzbergthal, past Rohrdorf Castle, and over a pass in the Weitergeberg into Bavaria, but in the late spring of '45 there was a series of avalanches and landslides in the mountains. The villagers say about a hundred feet of the top of the Schwarzberg itself collapsed into the valley and completely cut off the access, from north and south, to the Castle. The rear-guard troops who had fought their way up the valley—you can see signs of bullets and shrapnel scars on the walls of the Schwarzberghof it-self—were either wiped out by the landslides, or would have died of starvation in the castle after food supplies there gave out." I shuddered at the macabre picture I had conjured up.

"What a story!" breathed Crispin. "I came to Schwarzberg thinking I could make use of the area for the background of my next book. I never dreamed it would also provide me with an exciting plot."

"Do you always visit the background places you write about?" I asked with interest.

Crispin nodded.

"If I don't, I could easily make a mistake, ei-ther in my topographical description, or in my use of local legend, and if I did, believe me, Miss MacIntosh, I would have irate readers writing to me, pointing out my mistakes!"

Remembering the variety of backgrounds used in the Crispin novels, I said in amazement:

"Heavens! You must know Europe inti-mately! I can't think of a country you haven't written about."

"Scotland," he replied promptly. "That is one country I have never visited, although everyone who has been there tells me it is very beautiful, when it isn't raining!"

"It even rains in the Tyrol!" I said, scram-bling to my feet as heavy spots of wet spattered on my head. "We shall have to make a dash for cover."

Crispin stood up, grabbed my hand, and together we went racing back along the path we had come to the Gasthof, but by the time we reached the shelter we were both soaked to the skin.

I went hurrying up to my bedroom to change, feeling much more cheerful than I had for hours.

I had enjoyed my stroll with Jon Crispin. His questions had directed my thoughts from the events of the afternoon, and relieved the tension in my mind.

My first impression of him had been wrong. Jon Crispin was not such a cynical, unfriendly person as I had first considered him, I decided, as I stripped off my wet clothes.

Hadn't he proved this by his treatment of Hans Schmidt? I don't know how Liesl and I could have managed to carry the old man from the kitchen to his own quarters without Crispin's assistance, and it wasn't that we had had to ask for that assistance either.

Moreover, I am sure he had guessed how down in the mouth I had been feeling when he had tagged along with me on my stroll, and had deliberately, by his questions, turned my thoughts from the unhappy events of the afternoon to the happier times I had previously spent in Schwarzberg.

He had shown genuine interest in my sketch of the history of the valley, and I wondered if he actually would make use of it as an idea for a suspense plot.

I was sure he made a mental note of everything that was said to him in case it might prove of use to him in his writing, and from my observance of him, I knew too that he was deeply interested in all types of people.

I smiled at my reflection in the mirror as I stood there in my bra and pants.

Would Jon Crispin model one of his future female characters on me? I struck what I considered a suitably appealing, book-jacket-illustration pose and giggled.

How did the writer view me?

Did he see me as a prissy blue stocking, who quoted John Donne to put an inquisitive male in his place, or was his picture of me as a softhearted, Florence Nightingale type, who took care of tired, sick old men, or, I thought more hopefully, did he think of me as a romantic young girl who dreamed dreams of fairy tale castles in the Tyrol?

I tired of my childish fancies and posturings, and opened the wardrobe door to select a dry outfit.

What did it matter what Jon Crispin thought of me? We were chance acquaintances and after I left the Schwarzberghof we would never meet again.

I expelled a deep sigh as I started to dress.

All the same, it was fun to dream, and I would buy Jon Crispin's next novel and see if I could recognize myself!

Chapter Seven

I was sitting on the edge of the bed, rolling my finest pair of nylons carefully up my legs, when Liesl came bursting into the room.

She looked in a furious temper.

"Miranda! I could spit! Do you know what?" She flopped on the bed beside me.

"Mama telephoned just now to see how we were getting along without her, and Katz," there was no politeness in her reference to her step-father now—"and Katz, instead of telling her what had happened, and how everything is at sixes and sevens, actually said we were getting along beautifully without her, and although we all missed her, she was to stay on with her friends in Salzburg and enjoy the holiday she deserves."

"I think it was kind of him not to want to worry your mother," I reproved mildly.

"Kind of him!" gasped Liesl. "He doesn't know what it means to be kind. He might have thought about me a little! How does he expect me to cope with all the extra work here on my own? The place is swarming with reporters and casual visitors, wanting coffees and meals and keeping everyone back by asking for details of Schneider's death."

"You will manage, Liesl. You have done it before. I remember last time I was here, when your mother was ill for a few days, how very effi-

ciently you took over the running of the Gasthof."

"That was different," demurred Liesl sulkily.
"Papa was alive then, and he was always on
hand to help out, with the dishes and preparing
the vegetables. Work in the kitchen wasn't
beneath his dignity!"

I fastened my suspenders and stood up.

"Perhaps Herr Katz isn't used to running an
inn," I excused him. "Some men have no idea of
how much work goes on behind the scenes in
the kitchen."

"How do they think meals appear?" snapped
Liesl. "By magic?"

"Cheer up, Liesl! You are letting things get
you down and that isn't like you."

I stood in front of the mirror and pinned a
Celtic silver brooch, set with cairngorms, to the
shoulder of the pale blue courtelle shift I was
wearing.

"I tell you what," I went on, standing back to
admire the effect, "I shall give you a hand." I
turned to her with a teasing smile.

"I am more than just a pretty face!" I
laughed.

"You are pretty, Miranda!" Liesl surveyed me
critically. "I wish I was slim and tall and fair
skinned like you."

"And if you were, Franz probably wouldn't
spare you a second glance," I interrupted her.
"You wouldn't like that, would you?"

"Oh, no!" Liesl gasped in dismay at the
thought. "You know, Miranda," she went on, "I

shall be so glad when Franz and I marry, and he takes me away from here."

She stood up and smoothed the coverlet of the bed.

"Isn't it funny how things change? I never thought the day would come when I should be eager to leave Schwarzberg."

"Nor me!" I sighed. "This will be my last summer here, Liesl. With you gone, there will be no point in my returning, and as Mr. Crispin said to me, there's no use longing for yesteryear. No one can put back the clock, or keep time standing still."

"I wish one could!" Liesl picked up a bottle of scent from the dressing table and sniffed the contents.

"Herr Crispin is a writer, did you know?"

I nodded.

"I have started to read a paperback book by him." Liesl replaced the bottle. "I am not very sure if I like it. His hero is very tough, very ruthless—very like James Bond, you understand. There is not much loving."

"There is plenty of loving in the James Bond books!" I picked up the perfume phial and applied some to the pulses behind my ears, on my throat and at my wrists.

"I would not call that loving!" pooh-poohed Liesl. "Lusting perhaps. I would not like a man to treat me in that way. Franz tells me that these are books for men, and that men think differently of such things, but I am not so sure. I could not imagine my Franz as a James Bond!" she giggled. "Could you?"

I grinned back, shaking my head.

Liesl's Franz is small and plump and good-natured, not unlike what Liesl's father had been. I just could not in my wildest imaginings see him do anything ruthless or unkind.

"I could see Mr. Crispin himself in the part, though, couldn't you?" Liesl observed. "He even looks like the film James Bond, doesn't he? Mr. Paterson is much more attractive looking and conventional, don't you think?"

"I certainly could never see Niall doing some of the things James Bond does, if that's what you mean by conventional!" I agreed. "He is very *comme il faut*."

Our discussion of the merits and demerits of Crispin and Paterson was brought to a halt by Liesl.

"It can't be that time already!" she exclaimed, catching sight of my travelling clock. "Half past six! I must fly or dinner will be late."

She fled from the room, while I added the final touches of make-up to my eyelids before going down to the bar parlour for a pre-dinner apèritif.

Niall Paterson and Jon Crispin were already there. They both stood up as I came in and asked me to join them.

I did so gladly. I didn't want to be on my own and, in any case, it would be interesting to study the two men in the light of my recent talk about them with Liesl.

To my surprise, I noticed that Inspector Bauer and his assistant were sitting at a table in the far corner of the room.

"I thought the police had left," I remarked. "What brought them back again? Have there been new developments?"

Crispin shook his head.

"It seems I was mistaken when I told you they were leaving to return to headquarters, Miss MacIntosh. They were, in fact, leaving to climb the track up the mountain to examine the area from which they deduced Schneider fell."

"So they *did* believe what Hans told them!" I beamed with relief, for now that the police were prepared to accept the possibility that Rudi had been murdered, it really was not necessary for me to tell them what I had overheard, because beyond the fact that I could have told them, with certitude, that a murder had been committed, how else could I have helped them? I had been an aural, not a visual, witness to the crime, and nothing that I had heard would have given a clue to the murderers, and with this thought in mind, I soothed my still pricking conscience.

"I would not go so far as to say that the police took Hans seriously," said Niall didactically. "Inspector Bauer strikes me as a conscientious man. A suggestion has been made which might be remotely feasible, and for his own satisfaction he has decided to examine it. In this way, there could be no justification for future idle gossip that he had failed in his duty."

"He is quite right to overlook nothing," I agreed.

"Yes," nodded Crispin, "but even supposing Hans' story was correct, about Schneider telling him he had been pushed over the cliff, I don't see how an on the spot investigation would prove anything. Didn't the old man also remark that Schneider was taken by surprise by the action of his killer? A man taken by surprise is not likely to put up a struggle, so away goes any possible sign of murder."

Niall studied Crispin's face thoughtfully.

"You have it all worked out already, haven't you?"

"I am used to working out this type of thing," shrugged Crispin. "That's how I earn my living!"

"For goodness sake!" I protested angrily. "A man has been murdered and all you can think of is making use of the fact to entertain your public. And I thought you had some human feeling!"

The room had gone very quiet as I was speaking. Everyone from the Werners to Heinrich, the barman, was staring at me.

"Miranda!" Niall frowned with disapproval at my outburst.

"Miss MacIntosh!" Inspector Bauer had crossed to where I was sitting. "You used the word 'murder' just now as if you had no doubts about the fact." He looked down at me sternly.

"Tell me, Fräulein. What more did Hans Schmidt tell you after you had rushed him from my presence in such cavalier fashion this afternoon?"

Bauer spoke in German, but he must have understood English well to have picked up what I had been saying to Crispin.

I replied to him in his own tongue.

"You saw what the old man was like for yourself. He was in no fit state to say anything coherent after the way you all scared the wits from him with your shouting," I said feelingly.

"I used the word 'murder', Inspector, because I have known Hans for a long time, and I know when he is talking sense and when he rambles. I do not for one minute doubt that Schneider was still alive when he found him, and that Schneider managed to tell him what had happened. Surely, even you," I sneered, "must appreciate that the old man would not have the imagination to make up such a tale!" I echoed the words I had spoken to Jon Crispin earlier in the evening.

"The story still strikes me as fantastic," persisted Bauer. "Who would want to murder Schneider?"

"That is for you to find out!" I replied tartly.

Bauer sat down at our table.

"If murder has taken place, Miss MacIntosh, I assure you I will leave no stone unturned to find the murderer. Already I have spoken to Schneider's friends and acquaintances. None has a bad word for him. He was admired as a guide and mountaineer. He was a regular church-goer. He was a good son to his elderly widowed mother. He saved many lives on these mountains. If he had a weakness, it was for women, but no woman ever seems to have complained of his attention!"

"Perhaps one did this afternoon," suggested Heinrich, the barman, as he placed our drinks on the table.

"I was saying, not many minutes ago, that Schneider was well known as a lady killer! Perhaps someone reversed the roles," he joked grimly.

"We will be in a better position to judge what happened on the escarpment once we have examined the locale." Bauer ignored Heinrich's interruption. "Unfortunately, the rain and low cloud right down to the pine belt stopped us from doing so this afternoon, but we shall try again first thing tomorrow, if the weather lets us."

"Won't the rain wash away any traces, presuming there were traces, of how the accident took place?" Niall glanced at the window against which the rain was lashing with gusty fury.

"One never knows," shrugged the Inspector. "Even although I still maintain your old friend was rambling, Miss MacIntosh, I feel it my duty to search for the truth, and satisfy any doubts which may arise."

He accepted a cigarette from Crispin.

"I have gone as far as asking the local papers to insert a notice to the effect that I should like to interview anyone who was on or anywhere in the vicinity of the Schwarzberg. In this way, I hope to learn if anyone happened to see Schneider this afternoon, and if so, if they also saw if he was alone or with anyone, or if they even saw anyone near the spot where he fell from the hillside."

A cold trickle of sweat oozed down my spine.

Now, if ever, was my chance to speak, yet fear held my tongue. What if someone had noticed me! Would it not seem odd if I didn't speak up now? My mouth was dry with fear.

"I don't think you will have much luck in that direction." Heinrich was speaking, giving me time to pull myself together. "There was a special Saint's Day Procession in Schwarzberg village this afternoon. Most people, tourists and villagers alike, would be watching it, rather than roam the mountains."

Niall nodded. "I saw Mr. and Mrs. Werner there, and the Brauns," he mentioned another couple who were staying at the Gasthof, and with whom he and Crispin had been talking as I came into the bar parlour. "The Brauns have just arrived back, as a matter of fact. They waited to the very end."

"That is so," confirmed Irma Werner. "Johan and I went to watch the procession, but we came away early, unfortunately for us as it turned out," she pouted. "If we had stayed on, we would never have come across Schneider's body, and so would have escaped from any involvement in the affair."

Inspector Bauer turned to look at her.

"If you and your husband walked past the place where Schneider was lying, Frau Werner," he observed, "you must have returned to the Gasthof the long way round?"

"We had the afternoon in front of us," Werner interceded. "After the crowds at the festival, we felt like enjoying a long peaceful walk through the woods and meadows."

"Funny I didn't notice you at the procession,

Crispin," remarked Niall. "You would have got plenty of local colour there!"

"So I did!" replied Crispin blandly, "and some excellent cine shots to remind me of it, and of things I may have failed to notice at the time, like you, Mr. Paterson. You don't feature in any of the crowd scenes. Where were you standing?"

I didn't wait for Niall's reply.

Everyone else had volunteered to tell Bauer where they had been during the afternoon. It would have looked odd if I refrained from doing so, so I took a deep breath, licked the dryness from my lips and announced:

"I was on the lower slopes of the Schwarzberg this afternoon, Inspector Bauer, but I did not see another soul near me." I spoke the truth, even if I was deceiving.

"When did you go there?" he snapped. "What time?"

"I went out shortly after lunch."

"It was almost four when I met you coming out of the woods!" Niall exclaimed. "You couldn't have been roaming around all that time on such a sultry afternoon!"

"Of course, I wasn't!" I retorted. "I had taken a book with me, and went a little way up the mountain to look for a quiet spot to read and sunbathe."

"Why didn't you go to watch the procession like everyone else?" pried Bauer.

"Inspector, I have been in Schwarzberg often enough at this time. I have watched this procession five times! This year I decided to give it a miss and spend my time in the sunshine acquiring a tan, instead of being jostled around by mobs of sightseers."

"I see," Bauer nodded. "Tell me, exactly where did you find a suitable spot for your sun bath?"

I had to think carefully before I answered this question.

"It wasn't very far beyond the pine belt. I don't know exactly how far on. I wasn't paying much attention. I was merely meandering, and when I came to what I considered a pleasantly secluded spot, I sat there."

"You could find this place again?"

"I suppose so," I said, damning Bauer's persistence under my breath.

"Now, tell me, you seemed to have been walking for some time. Did you see other people on your way?"

"Of course, I didn't!" I snapped, my nerves on edge. "I would have told you so!"

"Not one single person? Not even in the distance? At least we know that Schneider was up the mountain at the same time as you."

"Are you implying that I saw Schneider and am not telling you I did?"

"Is it that the good Inspector thinks you were one of Rudi's conquests?" Irma Werner seemed amused. "Heinrich was telling us that he cast a wide net where his girl friends were concerned!"

"Oh!" I gasped at the implication. "How dare you!"

Irma shrugged. "It is the Inspector who dares. I only say what I think he has in mind."

I looked at Bauer, and from the expression on

his face, I knew that Irma had not spoken out of
turn.

I took a deep, shuddering breath.

"Don't let your hopeful imagination run away
with you, Inspector. I didn't know Rudi Schneider. I didn't even know what he looked like.
And," I drew another breath, "I certainly didn't
kill him!"

"If you insist on murder, you must expect me
to look for a murderer," he spoke blandly. "I
would be failing in my duty if I passed you over
for the part, without careful consideration,
wouldn't I?

"After all," he delivered his parting shot on
the stroke of the dinner gong, "you seem to be
one of the few people without an alibi?"

Chapter Eight

In spite of her protestations of inadequacy, the meal which Liesl produced that night was superb.

She offered a choice of marrow or beer soup. I opted, so did most of those in the dining-room, for the beer soup, which is made from heating ale over boiling water, adding blended cream, egg and sugar, and stirring the lot until the mixture thickens. Moments before it is served, it is seasoned with cinnamon.

The soup was followed by Veal Paprika or beef olives, with Apple Strudel for the sweet, and spiced coffee to finish off with.

When I had eaten, I went to the kitchen to congratulate Liesl on doing so well on her own, and to see if I could give her a hand with the washing up.

She was delighted with my praise, and my offer of help, so I wrapped an apron round my pale blue dress and set to work with dish mop and boiling water to clean the great pile of dishes stacked by the tub.

By the time we had finished, it was almost ten o'clock and I was feeling somewhat wilted, both from the unaccustomed task and the steamy heat of the kitchen. My hair was beginning to frizz, as it always does in a damp atmosphere, and the make-up I had so carefully applied before dinner had worn off.

Liesl, in spite of the fact that she had been

working hard all day, still seemed full of energy. She was busily stacking dishes on a tray in preparation for setting the tables in the breakfast room.

"Where do you get all your oomph, Liesl?" I asked tiredly as I doffed the apron, hung it on its peg in a cupboard behind the kitchen door and flopped down on a wooden trestle by the stove to rest my aching legs.

"I'm dead!" I gasped.

"Miranda!" exclaimed Liesl contritely. "I should not have let you do so much! Mama would be furious if she knew. One of her guests helping in the kitchen, indeed!"

"Come off it, Liesl!" I smiled. "I am your friend as well as your guest, remember. And even if I am tired, I enjoyed helping you. It was much better than sitting in the lounge, talking to a lot of strangers and wondering if any of them agree with Inspector Bauer that I killed Schneider!"

"What!" Liesl very nearly dropped the dish she was holding.

"He was trying to annoy me, I think, because I helped Hans escape from his clutches this afternoon," and I went on to tell Liesl of the conversation in the bar parlour before the dinner gong had rung.

"What rot!" said Liesl. "Of course, he was pulling your leg."

"Irma Werner didn't seem to think so. She saw what he was driving at before I did."

"Frau Werner is a very smart woman," said Liesl. "Do you know, she is editor of one of the

German fashion magazines? I believe, too, that she was once well known as a model."

"You would wonder what would bring someone like her to Schwarzberg, wouldn't you?" I said. "I would have thought Velden or Venice more her line of country as a holiday resort."

"My step-father knew Werner when he worked in Munich. I think it is because of him they decided to come here."

"By the way, talking of the Werners, didn't Mr. Crispin tell you they wouldn't be in for dinner tonight, because they were going to Innsbruck?"

Liesl nodded. "Yes. They had booked seats at the Exle Bühne and were all set to drive to Innsbruck, when the downpour started. You know, it is bad enough driving on the track to the main road in dry weather, with all the pot holes, and almost impossible when it rains, unless you know it well. My step-father advised them not to take the risk in case they got bogged down in one of the roughest parts."

"That was thoughtful of him."

Liesl shrugged. "They are his friends, aren't they?"

She lifted up the tray load of dishes and asked me to hold open the kitchen door. "I'll go and set the tables now, and that will be my work finished for the day, thank goodness!"

She flashed me a grateful smile. "You have no idea how much time you have saved me with your assistance."

I followed her from the kitchen, but she refused to let me help her in the breakfast room.

"No!" she said firmly. "You go and sit in the lounge, and when I have finished, I shall come there and join you, and we shall have a night-cap of hot chocolate together. How about it?"

"Like what we always used to have after the musical evenings." I smiled in memory.

Liesl looked sad as she nodded, remembering that her father had been the promoter of these gay evenings.

She went into the breakfast room, but as I turned to go to the lounge, I caught a glimpse of myself in the full-length oak-framed mirror in the hall, and decided to go up to my bedroom and renew my make-up and smooth down my hair without delay.

On my way up the narrow stairway, I met Jon Crispin coming down. He promptly re-treated to the landing.

When I thanked him, he smiled.

"Didn't you know it was supposed to bring bad luck if you passed someone on the stairs?" he asked. "I should hate to bring you ill chance, Miss MacIntosh."

Crispin looked most charming when he smiled, although his face, in repose, had the ruthless quality of the wild eagle.

As I reached the landing beside him, he eyed my shining face.

"You look a bit flushed," he observed. "What have you been up to this time?"

"Dancing the can-can, swilling champagne, and all in all, really living it up!" I smiled. "You have no idea what goes on in the kitchen of this Gasthof!"

"So that is where you were! When I asked, Joseph said you might be giving his sister a hand in the kitchen, but I thought he was being funny." He paused. "How about coming down for a drink before you turn in?"

"Sorry, Mr. Crispin. I have a previous engagement!" I refused the offer with a smile. "Thanks for asking me."

I went on to my room, where I carefully renewed my make-up before returning to the lounge.

The lounge was empty except for old Frau Habe, a permanent resident in the Gasthof. She looked up from her knitting to bid me "Good evening", but made no further attempt to converse, as her busy fingers clicked the needles together.

From the parlour bar next door, I could hear the murmur of voices and the clatter of glasses. The parlour is the hub of the social activity in the Gasthof. Guests only use the lounge when they want to have peace and quiet, and presumably this was why Liesl had arranged to meet me here. We wouldn't have to shout to hear ourselves speak, as we would have had to next door!

I picked up a magazine from a side table and thumbed through it. There was a long article about the flora of the Tyrol in it, with some excellent illustrations. I began to read it with interest. I had almost finished the article, when the sudden clamour of the front door bell startled me.

I wondered idly who could be arriving at the

Gasthof at this late hour, and in such wild weather conditions, before continuing with my reading.

When I had finished, I glanced at my watch. It was over half an hour since Liesl had said she would join me. Surely, it couldn't have taken her all this time to set the breakfast tables. I stifled a sleepy yawn. I was ready for bed. I hoped she wouldn't be much longer.

After another few minutes, I stood up and went along to the breakfast room. The tables were all set, but there was no sign of my friend.

I went to the kitchen, but only Joseph was there, sitting by the stove with a glass of milk and a piece of Apple Strudel. He was engrossed in a book, and knowing him of old, I knew better than to disturb him merely to ask for the whereabouts of his sister.

Had Liesl forgotten our arrangement and gone straight to bed after her tiring day's work, or had the ring I had heard on the door bell heralded the late arrival of friends of hers, whom she would be entertaining in her mother's private sitting-room?

I went back to the lounge and sat for a further ten minutes, by which time my eyes were so heavy I could scarcely keep them open. At last, I decided to call it a day.

Liesl had clearly forgotten about me, which was a pity. I had been looking forward to the promised cup of hot chocolate.

I said good night to Frau Habe, who sat on, knitting as if her life depended on it, and went upstairs to my bedroom.

I undressed, showered, put on a pair of cotton pyjamas and climbed into the outsize bed. I settled comfortably on the feather mattress and pulled the light-weight plumeau over my shoulder. I felt warm and snug and sleepy.

Outside the rain still spattered in gusts against the window panes, and the wind moaned like a banshee round the gable end of the house, forcing the long branches of the pear tree in the orchard to scratch and claw against glass and brickwork like an angry wild cat trying to force its way in.

I wondered drowsily how long the storm of rain would last as I pulled the plumeau further up over my ears to soften the angry weather sounds.

I was almost asleep, when there was a sharp, continuous rapping on the bedroom door.

I blinked sleepily.

The knocking was repeated.

"Miranda!" called Liesl in an urgent voice.

I sighed a deep sigh.

At long last, my friend had remembered her promise, and not finding me waiting for her in the lounge, she had come up to see if I was in my bedroom.

I switched on the bedlight, pulled my dressing-gown round my shoulders, and slipped out of bed to run across the floor and unlock the door.

"Miranda! I don't like disturbing you like this," Liesl came into the room, "but I had to come to you." There were unhappy tears welling from her eyes.

"That man!" she went on before I could say a

word. "Who does he think he is? Who does he think I am, to treat me like a serving wench in my own father's house!"

"Liesl! What on earth is it this time?" I heaved an exasperated sigh. I was beginning to feel the teeniest bit annoyed with my friend, the way she reacted to anything her step-father said or did.

"Two unexpected guests arrived tonight, without any warning. A man and his sister. Katz insisted we accommodate them, although I pointed out there was not a vacant room in the Gasthof.

"He said that in this weather, and at this hour of night, we could not turn guests from our door.

"I argued that what with police and reporters as well as our usual guests, we are bursting at the seams. I said—and was I not right, Miranda—?" she appealed to me. "I said these people have a car—it is only ten minutes' drive to Schwarzberg where there are other inns and hotels less busy than ours. I even offered to telephone to reserve accommodation, but Katz says no! He is an innkeeper, and an innkeeper does not turn guests from his door."

Liesl glared at me. "Bah! That man is no innkeeper! He worked in an office in Munich. Because he married an innkeeper's widow, that does not make him mine host!"

"Liesl, please!" I spoke quietly. "Your step-father is doing his best."

"He is trying to act the big man, that's what he is trying to do. He tells those strangers we can accommodate them. He sends Joseph, in the rain, to bring their luggage from the car. He orders me to prepare a hot meal for the travellers, and he tells me that for tonight Joseph and I must give up our rooms to the strangers!"

Liesl's eyes blazed. "He said Joseph could sleep with him and I," she choked on the next words, "I am to sleep on the old couch in the kitchen!

"Miranda, when I protested, do you know what he said? He said I would do as I was told. He was the head of the house now, and it was about time I accepted the idea.

"Miranda, he spoke so angrily to me then, I was afraid to disobey. I made these strangers their supper, and I prepared Joseph's room and my own lovely room for their use—it took me ages to put all my things safely away," she sobbed.

"But, Miranda, although I have done all that, I cannot—*will* not sleep on the couch in the kitchen! I would rather sit up in the lounge all night, than that Rosa and her sister, and Heinrich, especially Heinrich, should surprise me sleeping in the kitchen when they report for duty in the morning."

Tears of rage and mortification streamed down her cheeks.

"Katz says it is only for one night, but what matter? I will not have people think I am treated as a nobody here!"

"Poor Liesl!" I put a comforting arm round her. "I know how you must hate having to give up your own lovely room, but you needn't sleep in the kitchen. Look! The bed here could take half a dozen people in comfort. You run down and get your night things and come back and sleep here."

"No, I couldn't do that! That is not why I came to you."

"I know that, Liesl. But I am still insisting that you sleep here."

Liesl weakened. "My step-father would be furious if he found out."

"Why should he find out?" I asked. "Hurry and get your things, Liesl. I want to get to sleep."

"You really mean it, don't you?" Liesl's smile was bright as sun after rain. "Miranda darling, what would I do without you?"

"Sleep in the kitchen!" I giggled.

Liesl hurried off for her night clothes, and less than ten minutes later, after whispered "Good nights", we were both sound asleep in the big double bed, too tired out, after the long, disturbing day, to be disquieted by the eerie howling of the wind and the monotonous scratching of the pear tree branches against the window.

Chapter Nine

A cock crowing raucously from the orchard below, and a shaft of brilliant sunlight searing my still heavy eyelids, roused me from sleep early next morning.

I yawned and stretched, and with my movement Liesl, who had been sleeping curled up under the plumeau like a kitten, pushed aside the feather quilt and sat up.

She looked at the clock on the bedside table as she murmured a drowsy "Good morning".

"Heavens! It's quarter to six!" she exclaimed, and got out of bed. "I had better get dressed and downstairs before anyone else is up and about. Rosa will be bringing the milk in any time at all now, and I should not want her to see me stealing downstairs at this hour from the guests' side of the house."

She giggled. "She might think things, especially with so many handsome bachelors on the premises!"

She dressed hurriedly and tiptoed from the room, and I pulled the plumeau over me once more, and promptly fell asleep again, until roused by the breakfast gong!

I yawned and stretched once more, and slipped out of bed.

I looked out of the window to assess what the weather was before deciding on what I would wear that day. There were pools of water under the fruit trees in the orchard, and the meadows

looked sodden, but already the heat of the sun
was drying the big square flagstones of the garden path. The sky was delphinium blue with not
a cloud to be seen, and already the wisps of
white mist, which ringed the neck of the towering Schwarzberg like a tulle scarf, were evaporat-
ing.

I wondered what I would do with myself today.

With Liesl in charge of the Gasthof's workings
in her mother's absence, I knew she would have
no time to entertain me, and after what had
happened yesterday I had not the slightest desire to go wandering round the mountains on my
own, so I decided in favour of going for a day's
outing to Feldkirch, or perhaps even across the
Brenner to Vipiteno in Italy.

I put on a pencil-slim skirt, which I had made
for myself in MacIntosh tartan, and a white,
short-sleeved orlon pullover. I didn't bother
with much make-up, except for protection lotion
and a trace of lipstick, and picking up my handbag and anorak, I went down to breakfast.

The breakfast room was full, and I could not
spot a vacant place, until Niall Paterson called:

"Over here, Miranda! I managed to keep a
seat for you."

Grateful for his thoughtfulness, I went over to
join him.

The Werners and Jon Crispin were seated at
an adjoining table, and I wished them a polite
greeting as I passed.

"I have never seen the breakfast room so

busy," I said to Niall as I sat down. "Where has everyone come from?"

"Some from the village, some from the camping site, and all agog to hear the latest news," the lawyer told me.

"And what is that?" I said, as he passed me the basket of morning rolls.

"The Gasthof is having a real spell of notoriety!" said Niall.

"What do you mean?" I asked sharply.

"Haven't you heard?" he seemed surprised. "I thought your friend would have told you, and that was why you were late for breakfast."

"I slept in," I said tersely. "And now, please tell me what has been going on."

"There was a fire in Hans Schmidt's room in the middle of the night."

"No!" I gasped taken aback. "How did it happen? Was Hans hurt?"

"It seems he was lucky," said Niall. "He escaped with a few superficial burns on his legs, but, of course, he was badly shocked. He has been taken to hospital."

"Poor Hans! How did the fire start, do you know?"

"Inspector Bauer says the old man must have got out of bed in the middle of the night and knocked over a paraffin stove, which stood in the middle of the room. There was straw matting on the floor, which flared up like a torch and set the bedding alight. Hans was found lying there."

"I don't understand it." I shook my head. "Hans is lucky to be alive!"

"He wouldn't be alive if Wahl, Inspector Bauer's assistant, didn't suffer from insomnia, or so I hear. He had gone out for a walk after the rain stopped, and was passing the window of Schmidt's room, when he saw the blaze.

"He kicked the door open, whipped the burning bed clothes off the old man, and yelled for assistance." Niall helped himself to a roll. "It is terrible to think that if he hadn't happened to be there, Hans would be dead. The byres next to his dwelling must be stocked with hay, and you can imagine what an inferno there would have been."

I listened to what Niall was saying, but I was puzzled. I didn't see how Hans could have upset the paraffin stove, unless he had given it a really fierce shove. I had had a good look at it when we had put Hans to bed the previous afternoon, and had satisfied myself that it was not a danger to the old man.

Niall poured me a cup of coffee.

"You will realize now why we have so many casual people in for breakfast. A good few have come to rubberneck!"

"It's terrible!" I said, adding, because I could not help thinking it, "I wonder what can possibly happen next? Trouble comes in threes, don't they say?"

"Don't tell me you believe in superstitious fancies, Miss MacIntosh," Jon Crispin teased me from the next table.

"I think we all do, one way or another. It does not matter how sophisticated we think we are," I glanced at Irma Werner, whose beautifully manicured fingers were playing with the St. Christopher pendant she invariably wore round her neck, "we all have our pet beliefs."

"All the same, you know, there is often a good reason underlying some superstitions!"

"Like not walking under a ladder in case a bucket of water or a pot of paint falls on one," agreed Niall. "And not bringing hawthorn into the house, because it is known to give some people hay fever!"

"Yes. Things like that," I smiled, as I lifted my cup of coffee to my mouth.

"By the way, Miranda," Niall frowned, "where did you go off to last night? I was looking all over the place for you."

"I went to the kitchen to have a chat with Liesl after dinner." I ignored Crispin's raised eyebrows at this description of my washing up. "With her mother away and Liesl having to take charge in the kitchen, and supervise the housework, we cannot see as much of each other as we would like."

"How come you are so friendly with Herr Katz's daughter?"

"Liesl is not Herr Katz's daughter," I denied the relationship. "She is his step-daughter. Her own father was a darling! I miss him very much. Liesl is his double!"

"So you prefer your men small and dark!" teased Niall. "You have dashed my hopes! I was hoping your preference was for tall, fair-haired men."

"Some tall, fair men can be quite nice too!" I was enjoying the moment's flirtation, which took my mind off the bad news Niall had told me about earlier.

As we talked, the Werners finished breakfast and left the room, but Jon Crispin sat on, smoking a cigarette and jotting notes into the little red book he carried with him everywhere.

I glanced round at the other occupants in the room. Like Crispin, they appeared to have finished their meal, but were sitting on, possibly waiting to hear the latest news of the fire.

One person I did not see, although I expected to, was Inspector Bauer who, with his assistant, Wahl, the man who had rescued Hans Schmidt from his blazing room, had been spending the night at the Gasthof. Of course, in view of the change of weather, it was possible the Inspector had breakfasted early and set off for his investigation of the escarpment.

Niall recalled my wandering attention.

"Miranda, I am driving in to Innsbruck this morning. Would you care to come with me?"

I hesitated.

"As a matter of fact, I had decided to go much further afield today, to either Feldkirch or Vipiteno in Italy."

"Couldn't you change your mind?" he asked.

"Couldn't you?" I smiled. "I have acted the guide so often in Innsbruck during my former holidays here, I feel I would like to visit somewhere fresh."

"Please, Miranda," his smile was beguiling, "if you know the Tyrolean capital as well as you say you do, couldn't you show me around?"

I felt myself weakening.

"It's not much fun sight-seeing by one's self," he pleaded once more. "Do come with me!"

Still I hesitated.

"I tell you what," suggested Niall. "If you come with me to Innsbruck today, I shall drive you wherever you wish to go tomorrow. Is it a deal?"

"Yes!" I decided.

It would be nice not to spend the day by myself and Niall was pleasant company. With him I could enjoy myself and forget yesterday's horrible day.

One thing I couldn't forget, however, was Hans Schmidt's misfortune. I felt a wave of compassion for the poor old man. I was able to enjoy myself while he lay alone, and in pain, in an impersonal hospital ward.

"I shall come to Innsbruck with you, Niall," I went on, "but there is another condition."

"Yes?" Niall's eyebrows raised in a question, and at the adjoining table, Jon Crispin stopped writing, and his pen hung poised over his notebook, almost as if he was ready to record my next statement.

"Before we leave here, I shall find out to which hospital old Hans has been taken, and we can pay him a visit and see if there is anything he requires."

"Hans was taken to Innsbruck," Niall told me. "But need we visit him? I am one of those people who hate hospitals, and illness, and disease! I'm sorry, Miranda."

"You needn't be! Lots of people, especially men, feel as you do," I said. "However, you don't need to come into the ward with me. You could wait outside the grounds in the car."

"Very well," Niall's expression cleared. "I accept your conditions! How long will it take you to get ready to leave?"

"Ten minutes, at most. First, I must find where the hospital is situated, then I must tell Liesl we shan't be here for lunch, and finally," I said, "if we are going sightseeing, I had better put on my least elegant, but most comfortable, pair of shoes! From experience, I know that the Innsbruck pavements are particularly hard!"

Chapter Ten

Niall drove his squat, bronze-coloured Mercedes sports car carefully down the two kilometres of twisting, deeply rutted track which led from the Schwarzberghof to the main Telfs-Innsbruck highway.

In places, last night's downpour had washed away parts of the rough surface, leaving roots of the tall pine trees which flanked the path exposed, and in some cases dangerously protruding upwards.

"It is high time Katz did something about this entrance road," he ejaculated with annoyance, when a boulder about twice the size of a football suddenly came bouncing from the embankment and knocked against the side of the car, fortunately with no great force.

"It would cost a fortune to lay a decen track," I said. "Uncle Langheim used to say having such a tricky road to come put off a lot of casual guests, and only people who genuinely wanted to stay in a remote inn, and who were content with what it had to offer, would trouble to come. He said, in effect, it deterred undesirables and saved him the trouble of personally selecting his guests."

"That doesn't seem to me a way to conduct a business!"

"Perhaps not to your prosaic legal mind, Niall," I smiled, "but Liesl's father knew what he was talking about. People who came to the

Gasthof in his day were all people you felt you could be friendly with. Homely people. Happy people. Unsophisticated people. They came for the mountain walks, and the mountain scenery, and the mountain peace. And at night, there was always a happy sing-song round a warm fire." I sighed. "A pity it has changed so much. In the old days, we would never have had people like the Werners, so superior and intolerant of the other guests."

"How do I fit in?" For a second, my eyes met Niall's in the driving mirror.

"I can't place you," I said, turning to look at him. "When I first met you, you didn't strike me as the type who would enjoy a holiday in an out of the way place like this. You were in the Werner class, I decided."

Niall's eyes narrowed.

"You make me sound unfriendly."

"But you are not!" I said quickly. "My first impression was wrong. You get on well with everyone. Even Katz seems to mellow when you talk to him!"

"And that's something?" he laughed.

"That's certainly something!" I agreed.

Niall's hand, for a brief moment, pressed mine.

"I am glad of that, Miranda," he said quietly. "I am glad you changed your mind about me."

We came to the road junction, and now that we were on the main road, Niall was able to show me his car's paces.

I enjoy driving fast myself, but there were times when I felt like asking Niall to slow down just a little. Although I could judge that he knew what he was doing, I found his style rather hair-raising, and I wondered how many tyres and brake linings he burned up in a year!

We reached Telfs in no time at all, but once past the town, the traffic became dense. However, at this part the road is broad and straight, and there is plenty of room to pass the slow moving hay waggons, often ox-drawn, which form such a contrast to the fast moving cars which flash past them on the road.

We were soon racing through the lovely Sellrain Valley, which is a favourite place for Sunday picknickers from Innsbruck, and in under an hour I was directing Niall through Innsbruck, to cross the Inn River and find a parking place near the Hauptbahnhof, the principal railway station, which is fairly central for sightseeing.

"You can leave the car here for as long as you like," I told him. "We were lucky to get a place to park so early."

"Is the hospital near here?"

"We won't be able to visit Hans until the afternoon, Liesl informed me, so we shall do our sightseeing first."

"Had your friend heard how Hans was reacting?"

"He is still under sedation, so the hospital authorities informed her when she telephoned to ask about visiting hours. They also told her it was possible that no visitors would be admitted to see him today, because he is very weak. Much more so than had at first been thought."

"I am sorry to hear that." Niall took the key from the ignition lock. "Has he any relatives?"

"No one. His two sons were killed in the war, and his wife died of tuberculosis not long after. He had always worked for the Langheims, and although latterly he was not able to do very much, Uncle Langheim kept him on as an odd job man. He also let him have that room he lived in, so that the family could keep an eye on the old man, and the byreman who used to have the room took over Hans' cottage at the other side of the valley. It was an arrangement which suited everyone, because the byreman was married with a growing family."

Niall got out of the car and I followed.

"Where do we go from here?" he said, with a gay change of mood. "I must admit I am glad we are not starting our tour with a hospital visit."

"If we go along this road here, we come to the Triumphal Arch which is at the southern end of the Maria-Theresienstrasse."

"That's a street as famous as your Princes Street in Edinburgh, isn't it?"

"Equally famous, equally romantic and with equally good shops and tearooms," I agreed, "but, patriotic as I am, I think the view down the Maria-Theresienstrasse is far finer than anything you could see from Princes Street."

We halted at the archway and looked down on the view which countless holidaymakers have seen, photographed for themselves, and sent picture postcards of to destinations all over the world. I never fail to enjoy looking at it.

Right in the centre rises the graceful St.

Anne's column, topped by the marble figure of the Virgin Mary; on either side are the old houses and arcaded shops, and high above everything else, a dramatic back cloth, looms the great wall of mountain, whose crests, still covered with pristine snow, dominated the capital of the Tyrol.

Niall took some snaps of the view, as every good tourist should, and said the usual admiring remarks, but when I suggested walking down the street to visit the Goldenes Dachl, one of the "musts" of Innsbruck, he suggested instead that we go to one of the street's celebrated coffee houses and sample the equally celebrated Austrian pastries.

"We can do that later!" I protested.

"Now!" he said firmly, taking me by the arm. "Where shall it be, Erhart's or Hammerle's? Or have you another idea?"

"Schindler's," I decided, "but, Niall," I continued my protestations, "I thought you came to Innsbruck to see the sights!"

"Either you are very innocent, very unobserving, or very wise in the rules of the game, Miranda MacIntosh," he said, pressing his fingers more firmly round my wrist. "Which is it?"

"I don't know what you mean?"

"You are a very attractive young woman; the kind of woman I most admire. You are intelligent, well educated, good at mixing in company, able to take care of yourself—I want to get to know you better!"

I giggled.

"Niall! You sound as if you were reading a personal file from a marriage bureau."

"Marriage bureaux, and I mean a good marriage bureau, which takes its business seriously, are an excellent way for people to choose their life partners. The computer system will prove even better."

"Niall! You don't believe that for a moment!" I gasped.

"Miranda, if you had to deal with as many broken marriages as I have to, you would agree with me that there must be saner ways of choosing a life partner than mere chemical attraction."

"Niall Paterson, you are pulling my leg! You are not nearly so cold-blooded as you would have me believe." I smiled as we entered the tearoom of our choice and sat down at a vacant table.

"The trouble with you," I went on, placing my handbag and the anorak I had been carrying on the bench beside me, "is that you have been too busy or too careful to let yourself fall in love. Once you do, you will not give a damn whether the object of your affections is blonde or brunette, tall or small!"

"Won't I?" He looked at me with his blue, blue eyes and something in his gaze made me look away, and I felt my cheeks redden. "Perhaps not, after all," he said softly.

I picked up the menu card. I had to do something, say something, which would break the spell of the moment.

"I like my coffee very strong and with lots of cream, how about you?"

Niall was still looking at me, as if he had never seen me before, and it gave me the oddest feeling.

"I like my coffee 'black as sin and hot as hell'," he quoted, with a return to his normal, friendly manner.

I wondered if it was by accident or design he had missed out the third ingredient from the quotation, and as if he had read my thoughts, he added:

"And yes, Miranda, if I knew what I was talking about, I might also say 'sweet as love'." He smiled and the awkwardness of the last few minutes passed off.

A trolley, laden with every conceivable type of Austrian pastry, was wheeled over to our table and I tried hard to decide on whether to take a Nusskipfel, a Sachertorte or a Punschkrapfen. Niall had no hesitation in deciding on a Mohnstrudel, a thin, sweet pastry filled with rolled poppy seeds in a mixture of sugar and honey, and I decided to follow his example.

In between mouthfuls, Niall asked me about my hometown, my parents, my ambitions.

"I hope to get a job with the World Health Organization in Geneva," I told him, "either that or with the Foreign Office. That's why I travel abroad so much—to perfect my knowledge of languages."

"You speak German very well," he assured me. "You should have no difficulty getting the work you want, but it seems odd to hear a woman talk of careers, and never marriage. Most girls I have met put finding a husband high on their list of priorities."

"Perhaps that is what has put you off women!" I twinkled. "Man prefers to be the hunter." I sipped the coffee through its thick cap of cream.

"And now, we have talked enough about me. I think it is high time you told me about yourself! Where you come from—"

"London," he interrupted promptly.

"You may work in London, but your accent tells me you don't belong there."

"My accent!" he appeared taken aback. "What do you mean?"

"I have been trying to decide if you were a Geordie or what. You aren't Scots or Irish, in spite of your name. I am pretty sure you don't come from Wales. You definitely aren't a Londoner—so, appease my curiosity. Where do you come from?"

"My father travelled about a great deal. We were never very long in one place. I daresay my accent is a hotch potch of all the accents in the places I lived in!"

"Are your parents still alive?"

"No." He spoke the word abruptly. "Look, if you are finished, Miranda, let's get on with our sightseeing, shall we?" He signalled the waiter.

I said no more. My question about his parents seemed to have disturbed him. Perhaps they had died recently, and he was still mourning for them.

We spent the rest of the morning sightseeing, but at half past one we called a halt and returned to the Stuberl for lunch.

Before going on from there to the hospital to inquire about Hans, Niall insisted on taking me to a shop in the Maria-Theresienstrasse arcade, to choose a souvenir for me.

"You have been the best guide I could have wished for. I want to say thank you," he said as he studied the goods in the show counters.

"I enjoyed every minute of it, Niall. It was fun showing you round."

In spite of my protestations, he made me the gift of a fine silver pendant, to which was attached a large coin with the likeness of the Empress Marie Thérèse, after whom the main thoroughfare in Innsbruck had been named.

After he had paid for the pendant, Niall insisted on fastening it round my neck 'for luck', as he said.

I was to need all the luck that charms and amulets could possibly bring in the near future, but I had no inkling of the dark hours ahead as I fingered the silver talisman.

"This will always remind me of today," I thanked Niall. "It has been fun, hasn't it?"

"It has been an experience for me," he said quietly, as we retraced our steps to where his Mercedes was parked. "Where do we go from here?"

"The hospital," I reminded him. "We were going to visit old Hans, remember?"

"Yes," he said shortly. "We must not forget what we came to Innsbruck to do, must we?"

He unlocked the doors of the car, and seconds later we were nosing through the traffic of the busy streets.

Chapter Eleven

Sad news waited for us at the hospital.

Old Hans had died during the morning. He had never recovered consciousness.

"It was the best way," said the nurse who talked to me. "He was very old and very frail, and in his condition, the burns he received last night would have taken a long time to heal, and it would have been months before he would have left the hospital bed, if ever."

I was upset by the news, but Niall was indifferent, although he tried to sympathize with me. Hans' death dimmed the brightness of the day for me, but worse was to come.

When we arrived back at the Schwarzberghof, we could hardly find a space for the car, there were so many other vehicles packed into the courtyard.

"I wonder what is going on?" Niall scowled as he was forced to occupy a rather muddy space outside the byres.

"They sometimes have receptions and weddings and the like." I was equally puzzled. "But Liesl did not mention anything of the nature."

"It looks more like a police convention," said Niall grimly, indicating a van, a Land-Rover and a saloon car with the word "Polizei" on them.

"You don't think Inspector Bauer is on to something, do you?"

"What do you mean?"

"Why—Rudi Schneider's murder, of course!

He might have found evidence of sorts when he went to examine the scene this morning."

"Nonsense!" said Niall sharply. "I wish you would stop harping on about a murder. You almost sound as if that's what you wanted Schneider's death to be!"

I opened my mouth to tell Niall what I knew, but at that moment Jon Crispin emerged from the inn, and came striding towards us.

"Did you know poor Hans is dead?" I asked him. "We have newly come from the hospital."

"The news was telephoned here," Crispin spoke curtly. He looked at me with a curiously impersonal look.

"The police will be glad you have returned. They have been looking for you."

"What do the police want with Miranda?" demanded Niall.

"They will tell her that for themselves." Crispin's voice was decidedly unfriendly. "Here is Inspector Bauer now!"

"Ah, Miss MacIntosh! So you have come back. We were beginning to wonder about that."

"What is all this about?" I demanded in perplexity. "I didn't know we were not supposed to leave the Inn."

"I think you had better come with me, Miss." The Inspector took my arm, but not in the same affectionate way which Niall had been holding it for the better part of the day.

The way in which the policeman gripped gave me the feeling he was taking me to prison, and not to a room in an inn for a friendly chat.

"Bauer!" Niall's voice, sharp and commanding, made the Inspector stop and turn round.

"Mr. Paterson?" his tone asked a question.

"Why do you wish to speak privately with Miss MacIntosh?" Niall challenged him.

"It is police business."

Niall's eyes narrowed.

"Police business? What has Miss MacIntosh been up to that the police should be interested in her?"

"You will no doubt learn that in due course," replied Bauer. "Come, Miss MacIntosh."

"Miranda," Niall gave me an encouraging look. "I do not know what this is all about, but remember, my dear, I am a lawyer as well as a friend. If you need me I shall be ready to help."

"I have the feeling you will have to implement that offer in the very near future, Paterson," I heard Crispin say as Bauer piloted me through the Inn to the sitting-room, which was empty save for the officer who had been with Bauer the previous evening, and another boyish-looking man in uniform.

"Sit down, Miss MacIntosh."

The Inspector indicated a chair which directly faced the window. He himself stood with his back to the view, looking directly down at me.

Seconds passed, and no further words were spoken. The only sounds in the room were the ticking of the carved cuckoo clock in the corner, the even, heavy breathing of the three men, and my own shallower, more nervous breaths.

I gripped the wooden arms of the chair in which I was sitting.

"Inspector Bauer, what is all this about?"

"Don't you know, Fräulein?"

My mouth dried up with tension. Of course! Someone had seen me on the Schwarzberg the previous afternoon, and at a spot much nearer the scene of the accident than I had admitted.

I swallowed hard.

"I suppose it's about Schneider's death?"

"Why did you push him over the cliff, Miss MacIntosh?" Bauer posed the question so mildly that, for a moment, I did not grasp its import.

Then, as I appreciated that I was being charged for the guide's murder, my facial muscles tensed in a spasm which made my jaw drop, leaving me gaping wide-mouthed and startle-eyed at the police inspector.

"Well, Miss MacIntosh?" Bauer looked coldly down at me, probing for his answer.

I was still speechless with shock at the accusation.

Seconds passed.

Unexpectedly the silence was broken by the gay, cheeky salutation of the cuckoo in the clock as it popped out to announce the hour.

By the time it had finished informing us in its raucous way that it was already four o'clock, I had managed to pull myself together.

"I don't know what you are driving at, Inspector Bauer," I snapped, pushing myself up from the chair and glaring angrily into his face.

"If you think you can find an easy solution to

your murder case by selecting a foreign scape-
goat, you are very much mistaken!

"I did not know Rudi Schneider. I still do not
even know what he looks like. I think you must
be quite out of your mind even to associate me
with him!"

The Inspector's next words completely
shocked me.

"We have proof that you were together yesterday afternoon, Fräulein," he said coldly.
"There is no use denying it."

"But I do deny it!" I cried, stamping my foot
like an angry child. "I never set eyes on Schneider in my life!"

"So?" the Inspector's brows were raised in a
disbelieving arch. "You deny knowing Schneider."

"Of course, I do!"

"Do you also deny being up on the Schwarzberg yesterday afternoon?"

"No! I told you I was there."

"You told us, young lady, that you only went
a little way beyond the tree line. We have proof
that you went much further up the mountain.
Much, much further!"

"I couldn't tell you within yards how far up I
went," I prevaricated. "All I was interested in
was finding a pleasant, secluded spot to lie and
sunbathe, where I would not be disturbed by
casual hill walkers. I didn't have to measure the
distance in feet to be able to find my way back
to the main paths!"

"Ah! Fräulein! That is the point. Your nice,

secluded spot for sunbathing was not at all far from the main path, was it?"

I felt dizzy, and my legs began to tremble.

"I think you had better sit down again, Miss MacIntosh." The Inspector spoke not unkindly.

I was glad to follow his advice.

"I tell you, I didn't kill Schneider!" My voice was the merest whisper.

"Miss MacIntosh, when Wahl and I were studying the ground in the vicinity of the spot from which Schneider was supposed to have slipped," he emphasized the word "slipped", "we found some interesting traces."

I couldn't keep my eyes from his mouth, which formed each damning word he uttered with eloquent precision.

"In a secluded hollow, directly under the point of the escarpment from which Schneider fell, we found the label from a bottle of sun oil, a bunch of daphne which had been very recently plucked and," he hesitated before telling his final proof of my presence at the fateful spot, "a strand of pink orlon caught in one of the stems of rhododendrons."

I kept staring wordlessly at him.

He hammered home the nails of his evidence.

"Joseph Langheim tells me that this was a favourite spot where you and his sister often went to sunbathe, which confirms my idea that you went there deliberately.

"The label from the sun oil fits over the unlabelled bottle of the same oil we found on your dressing table.

"Mr Crispin said that when you arrived back

at the Inn yesterday afternoon, you were somewhat dishevelled, and the pullover you were wearing was torn.

"The orlon thread we found exactly matches the strand of pink we found on the bushes and—"

"All right!" I shouted. "I won't deny that I was at that particular spot—I was! I should have told you!"

"Then why didn't you?" Bauer asked sternly.

"Don't you see?" I pleaded. "I did not want to get involved!"

"Involved in what?"

I bit my lip.

"I knew if I reported Schneider's death I would be questioned and questioned—"

"And you didn't want that, did you, Miss MacIntosh?" said Bauer craftily. "You knew where the answers would lead! But we would have been sympathetic, Miss MacIntosh. We would have understood.

"Schneider interrupted you when you were sunbathing, didn't he? He had a reputation where women were concerned. He tried to make advances to you. You resisted and ran away. He followed you and caught up with you. In the ensuing struggle, you accidentally pushed him over the cliff—"

"No! No!" My voice shrilled in piercing denial. "It wasn't like that at all. It wasn't. I'll tell you—"

But Inspector Bauer didn't listen.

"I could have sympathized with what you did, Miss MacIntosh," he looked at me sternly, "if you had not tried to save your own skin at the cost of Hans Schmidt's life. If you hadn't set fire to that poor old man's room in an attempt to keep us from hearing what other words the dying Schneider told him."

I felt as if my reason was deserting me as the Inspector went on:

"Mr. Crispin told us you seemed interested in the oil stove, when you helped settle the old man in his room, and that you had given Hans enough brandy to dope him!

"Miss MacIntosh, you will be charged not only with the murder of Rudolf Schneider, but also with being involved in the death of Hans Schmidt!"

Chapter Twelve

I closed my eyes to shut out the accusing faces of Inspector Bauer and his assistants.

I was dreaming, I assured myself. This was not happening to me! I would force myself awake and escape the nightmare.

I opened my eyes and the faces were still there, with their stern, pitiless gaze directed towards me. My frightened fingers played with the silver medallion which hung round my neck; the medallion Niall had given me as a lucky souvenir of a happy day.

I shuddered. Maria Thérèse had brought me very little luck and my happy day was ending in disaster.

"Do you wish to get in touch with the British Consulate in Innsbruck?"

Bauer's formal question penetrated the swirling haziness of my mind. I forced myself to attention, and as the shock of Bauer's unexpected accusations began to wear off, and I began to think clearly for myself again, anger rather than fear filled me, and sharpened my thinking powers.

"No, Inspector. I don't think there is any need to do that. You have made an error of judgement, but it is not a mistaké which would do your career any good if it was to be publicized."

It was the turn of the Inspector and his men to be taken aback.

"If you would be good enough to ask Mr. Paterson, who is a lawyer, and also a friend of mine, to join us, and also Mr. Crispin, who seems to have been responsible for some of your accusations, I will not merely refute your charges, but also tell you certain facts which I should have told you much earlier."

The men looked at me as if they thought I was mad.

"Fräulein! You cannot deny our evidence," defied Bauer.

"All I ask," I said firmly, "is that you bring the two Englishmen here to listen to my story, and to substantiate parts of it."

Bauer hesitated, then signalled the uniformed officer to do as I asked.

"What is wrong?" demanded Niall, as he strode ahead of Crispin into the room. "What has been going on here?" He came to stand by my side.

"Niall, Inspector Bauer has suggested that I killed both Schneider and old Hans."

Niall stiffened. "That is utterly ridiculous!"

"No," I denied. "They have made out a very strong case against me, with the evidence supplied them by Mr. Crispin there, among others."

I looked across at Crispin with scorn in my eyes, and as he looked back at me, I noticed his brow wrinkle in doubt.

Niall looked from one man to the other.

"What evidence have you against Miss MacIntosh? I hope you said nothing, Miranda, that would incriminate yourself."

"My mistake was in thinking I could get away

with ignoring murder," I said simply, and my words caused instant attentive reaction from my audience.

"If I had told you, Niall, the reason for my dishevelled appearance yesterday afternoon, I would not be in the position I am now."

Niall started and Jon Crispin moved a pace nearer.

"When Crispin told the Inspector about my torn pullover, and the Inspector found that I had been within yards of the cliff from which Schneider was pushed yesterday afternoon, he decided that Schneider had surprised me when I was sunbathing, made unwelcome advances and was pushed over the escarpment in my ensuing fight for honour," I spoke grimly.

"If that had been the case, he was prepared to deal leniently with me, but he decided that I had been at great pains to conceal my part in the affair. At such pains," I looked scornfully at the Inspector, "that I would stoop to murdering a poor, defenceless old man, who might or might not have known I was responsible for Schneider's death!"

"My God!" Niall looked round as if he couldn't believe what he was hearing.

"Again," I fixed the novelist with a contemptuous eye, "it was Crispin who gave him the idea I might be involved in last night's fire!"

Niall's fists clenched and he took a step towards Crispin, but I put out a hand and drew him back.

"No, Niall. Crispin was only using what he

would call his powers of deduction, or should I say detection?" I mocked.

"You are wasting time, Miss MacIntosh," interrupted Bauer harshly. "I should like to hear what you have to say to refute my charges."

"Rudi Schneider was murdered," I began, and ignored the sharp intakes of breath of all present. "I was there when it happened!"

I licked my lips. "I know I should have told my story right at the outset, but—" I hesitated, "I am human enough to make excuses for myself—I did not want to be involved!"

"If you were present when a murder was committed, Miranda, you were involved," Jon Crispin spoke softly. "No matter whether the murder had nothing to do with you, it was your duty to come forward and name the guilty parties."

"But that's just it!" I sighed despairingly. "I don't know who they were."

"They?" rapped out Bauer. "Was more than one person there?"

"I think there were two. There might have been others."

"What did these men look like?" he rapped out. "Describe them to me."

"I can't!" I cried. "I never once saw them!"

Everyone seemed to be trying to ask me questions at the same time.

"Please!" I implored. "Please listen! I was up on the Schwarzberg sunbathing at exactly the spot the Inspector found evidence of my presence.

"I must have fallen asleep. I was awakened by

a fearful screech. Before I could pull myself together to go and see what had happened, I heard two men talking on the escarpment over my head. They must have been only ten or fifteen feet away from me, but I could no more see them than they could see me, because of the overhang."

Crispin let out a long, low breath.

"Did you hear what they said?"

I shivered.

"Oh, yes. I'll not forget these words in a hurry! One said, 'There goes one who will not trouble us again.' He actually laughed after he spoke." I looked round my audience. "Or perhaps that was the other man, who replied, 'You acted very cleverly, my friend. Rudi's death will appear to be an unfortunate accident. A careless slip of the foot on a treacherous path.' Then the other added, 'Dead men tell no tales!' "

My shaking fingers twisted my medallion round and round as I continued:

"Do I need to tell you how terrified I was? Do I need to tell you I dived for hiding among the rhododendrons, not taking time to look for bottle labels, and not giving a damn if I did tear my pullover as I wriggled to the middle of the shrubbery for cover?"

Niall stared down at me with glassy eyes, and it was Crispin who came to put a steadying hand on my trembling shoulder.

"Why didn't you tell us this story before?" demanded the Inspector harshly.

"I was frightened and I did not want to be in-

volved, as I have told you." I looked at them all
for understanding.

"Don't you see? As I crouched in those
bushes, afraid for my own life, up there on the
mountain it came to me that if I told this story,
not only might I be held up in Austria indefinitely, as a possible witness in a murder case,
but I might even be murdered myself! These
men who had committed one murder would
have no compunction in eliminating someone
else who might betray them." I looked around
the faces which were focused on me.

"I would have no chance to guard myself!
These men could even be people I knew well.
People from the village—people living at the
Gasthof. Oh, don't you see?" I pleaded vehe-
mently. "Silence was my only safeguard, for how
could even you, Inspector Bauer, ensure my security when you had no idea from whom I had
to be protected."

Jon Crispin's grip on my shoulder tightened.

Inspector Bauer paced up and down the room.

"It is a good story, Fräulein. It gives you an
excusable reason for your reticence, but you
have nothing to substantiate it."

"You have nothing to substantiate your own
ridiculous theory!" I retorted with spirit. "You
could offer not one fact which would satisfy an
Austrian court that I had anything to do with
Rudi Schneider's death!"

Niall nodded in agreement.

"What is more, Inspector Bauer, as far as
your extraordinary charge about my setting fire
to poor old Hans' room, not only do I deny it,

knowing it to be utterly false, but for your satisfaction, if that is the right word to use, I can prove that I could not possibly be responsible!"

Inspector Bauer's eyes narrowed.

"Inspector, I have witnesses who can vouch for the fact I was never on my own for more than a few seconds last night!"

"The fire was raised in the small hours of this morning, as well you must know, Miss MacIntosh. Don't tell me," there was a sneer in the Inspector's tone, "that you had someone with you at three o'clock this morning?"

"As it happens, I did," I told him exultantly.

My words took everyone present by surprise.

Niall's jaw dropped and Crispin's fingers convulsively pierced through the thin wool of my sweater as they closed with a painful grip on my poor shoulder.

"Liesl Langheim shared my bed last night," I explained to my gaping audience. "She had had to give up her own bedroom for the use of a late arrival at the Inn, and since she did not relish the idea of sleeping on a makeshift bed in the kitchen, she came to me."

The glare in Niall's eyes vanished and Jon Crispin's pressure on my shoulder eased.

As for the Inspector, it was obvious from his facial expression that I had completely taken the wind out of his sails!

Once more he started his angry pacing of the room.

"I was so sure it must be you!" he scowled. "It all seemed to fit in. Young Joseph Langheim told me you knew your way about the place as well as he did. He said you were bound to know there was a way into Schmidt's quarters from the loft which leads from the byre. He told me that when you were younger, the three of you—Joseph, Liesl and yourself—often used to play up there."

I looked at him, thinking how many people he must have questioned during the course of the day from Crispin to young Joseph, and heaven knew who else.

"What makes you believe that entry to Schmidt's room was gained through the loft?" asked Niall in his best legal manner.

Bauer switched his attention to the lawyer.

"Surely, you realize that the officer who spotted the blaze, and who broke into the room to get it under control so promptly, was not outside Schmidt's quarters by accident?

"In case there was something to the old man's story, to be on the safe side, I decided to keep him under surveillance. My man was watching his door all night, and that is why we are sure no one could have entered by it. There had to be another way."

"I see." Niall compressed his lips in thought. "So now, Inspector, it must be obvious to you, in view of Miss MacIntosh's alibi for the time of the fire, that she could have had nothing to do with it. And from that it follows, doesn't it, she could have had nothing to do with Schneider's death either, since the attempt on Schmidt must have been made by the guide's murderer to prevent him from passing on any further knowledge he might have had of who had caused the guide's death."

"That is the obvious conclusion," agreed Bauer reluctantly, but I had the feeling he was not too pleased about the turn of events.

He had thought he had solved his murder case neatly and expeditiously. Now he would have to start looking for a different suspect, and with very little hope of success, unless his appeals to the public to tell him if they had seen anyone on or near the Schwarzberg about the relevant time met with success.

He relit his pipe, and as he sucked noisily on the stem, he looked across at me searchingly.

"It seems I was wrong about you, Miss Mac-Intosh," he spoke between puffs. "But had you come to me with your story in the first place, you would not have been subjected to this unpleasantness."

"I know," I agreed unhappily. "If I had, old Hans might still be alive."

"You can't blame yourself for that!" Crispin spoke sharply. "He could have been given no more protection than he had, could he, Bauer?"

"No," agreed the Inspector, and the awful feeling of guilt, which had been weighing me down since I had learned the reason for the attack on Hans, faded. "No," he repeated. "Even if you had told us your evidence sooner, it would not have saved Schmidt. I had him under safe surveillance, as I thought. I would have done no more."

I drew a long sigh of relief.

"Can I go now?" I asked hopefully, longing to

get out of the stifling atmosphere of the living-room, but Bauer shook his head.

"No, not just yet," he replied to my disgust. "There are a few more questions I should like to ask you.

Chapter Thirteen

Before proceeding with his interrogation, Bauer rang the service bell, and when Heinrich the barman, who sometimes doubled as waiter, appeared he ordered coffee for all of us.

"This should help to clear our heads," he joked grimly, when Heinrich reappeared with the order.

Wahl poured the liquid into the cups, and the uniformed policeman, whom Bauer addressed as Decker, handed them round.

Crispin, who during the first interview, had hovered by my side like a guardian angel, went over to sit beside Bauer, while Niall Paterson drew up a chair alongside mine.

Niall was not in a talkative mood. There was a faraway look in his eyes, as if he was going over in his mind all that had been said up to now, and was weighing it for legal significance, and I decided not to interrupt his train of thought.

Crispin was scribbling in the notebook he always had with him. He was getting plenty of material to work on this afternoon, I thought, with a flicker of annoyance. How lacking in feeling he must be to make use of other people's discomfiture!

I shot him an angry glance. I wished now that I hadn't insisted on him coming here to listen to my refutal of the evidence he had led against me.

At the same time, my annoyance cooled to puzzlement. I had to admit I had been glad of his presence. It had been Crispin who, with his steadying hand on my shoulder, had comforted me when my despairing spirits had been at their lowest ebb.

What had made him champion me in these moments? The usual Englishman's natural reaction to help the underdog?

I continued to look at him, puzzled.

I could not understand him at all. One minute he could be friendly, the next one, scathing. He was not a man one could get to know easily; not a man I would have said was my type, for all his physical attraction. Although I had enjoyed the walk we had taken together the previous afternoon, I had had no desire to pursue the acquaintanceship, because the enjoyment had been mingled with discomfort.

Jon Crispin might earn a living from his pen, but he was not a dreamer. He even seemed to despise dreams. He did not want to put a sugar coating on life.

He was a realist where I was a romantic and from reading his books, I gathered there was no room for sentiment in his life.

Moreover, I stirred uncomfortably in my chair, when I had been with Crispin, and even now, when I was in the same room as he was, I was very much aware of him physically, and from the way I had seen Irma Werner, and even Liesl, eye him from time to time, I sensed they, too, were aware of his masculinity.

I had an idea he looked on women much as the heroes of his books looked on them, as mere

passing fancies, and I disliked the idea. At the
same time, I could not imagine Jon Crispin
choosing a wife, if the idea of marriage ever oc-
curred to him, by computer, as Niall Paterson
had suggested was the ideal way to select a
mate.

Niall and Jon.

I looked from one to the other through the
sweep of my long eyelashes. I could not imagine
two men more different in appearance or out-
look, nor two men whose views of love were so
extreme and remote from my own.

John Donne, the seventeenth century poet and
philosopher, had known a thing or two when he
wrote—

> "Just such disparitie
> As is twixt Aire and Angells puritie
> Twixt womens love and mens will ever be!"

As if aware of my quizzical gaze, Crispin
looked up from the notes he had been making.

For a second our eyes met, and held, and as
we thus looked at each other, it seemed to me
that once more I could feel the warm, encouraging grip of his fingers on my shoulder, and my
own hand went up and touched the place where
his hand had rested.

As I did so, I could have sworn that an
amused gleam sparked in Jon Crispin's eyes, and
in confusion, I hurriedly averted my gaze and
began to chatter to Niall Paterson, who had
been sitting silently staring at his shoe-caps, as

if the brightness of their polish had mesmerized him into a trance.

"Niall. Isn't it a shame that the delightful day we were enjoying should have ended like this!" The words came breathlessly. "I am terribly sorry that my stupidity dragged you into the affair."

"That's the trouble with women," he spoke peevishly. "They just don't think ahead! If you had had the good sense to tell me the truth about why you were in such a state when I met you coming from the woods yesterday, you would have saved me, yourself, and the police, a great deal of trouble!"

The sharpness of his rebuke took me by surprise. I had been expecting a little friendly understanding and sympathy, and I was confused at his attitude.

"Miranda was a coward on instinct," Crispin blandly excused me, "and women are noted for obeying their instincts! Quite right, too. Apparent cowardice is not necessarily a moral weakness, you know. Just the natural desire for self-preservation! Don't tell me you wouldn't have acted in precisely the same way if you had thought you could have got away with it!" he mocked.

Niall shot him an angry look, but before he could frame a suitable reply, Inspector Bauer, who had been following our remarks with interest, although we had been talking, for a change, in our native English, laid aside his coffee cup and agreed with Crispin's remarks in his own tongue.

"Jah! Jah! It takes either a brave man or a fool to deny this instinct to run away from danger. But enough of philosophizing." His tone became briskly official. "Let us get back to business."

He stood up and came over to me.

"Miss MacIntosh," he looked down at me, "let us consider your account of what happened yesterday on the Schwarzberg. These men you spoke of, are you quite sure that you did not catch even the slightest glimpse of one or other of them?"

I shook my head.

"But surely, Fräulein, you must have seen something! An idea of the height they were? Perhaps even the colour of the clothes they wore? The place where you were hiding was immediately beside the track down which they had to pass!"

"I know, Inspector. They passed so close to me, I could have put out my hand to touch them, but close as they were, I assure you I saw not even a fleeting vision of them. I was very glad of the density of the bush in which I was hiding, Inspector, because I knew, as I crouched there, that if I could not see them, they certainly could not see me, and that was all I was worrying about at the time."

Bauer pursed his lips together and went thoughtfully back to sit beside the coffee table.

"This gets us nowhere!" he scowled angrily. "If we had just one clue to go on. One clue!" His clenched fist came down on the table, making the tray of dishes clatter noisily. "Here we have two murders, and not one single pointer as to who could have committed them!" He groaned.

"Fräulein MacIntosh," Wahl, the assistant, spoke. "You said, did you not that you heard these men speak? Do you think you would recognize the voices if you heard them again?"

Inspector Bauer perked up visibly at this hopeful suggestion.

I fingered my pendant pensively.

"I doubt it, but if it is anything to go on, although in this area I don't think it is of much help, one of the speakers was definitely from Bavaria, judging from his accent. The other," I frowned in recollection, "I am pretty sure he did not come from anywhere near this region, but I couldn't place his accent. From the North, I would have said, by its harshness."

The Inspector sighed.

"That does not get us very far, does it, but at least, it is something. Unless you remember something else?" he added hopefully.

"How about the motive for the crime?" I asked. "Schneider was not pushed over the cliff for no reason."

"Jah!" nodded the Inspector. "If we find out why, it might help, but very often, one cannot find the 'why' without having a good idea of the 'who'."

Once more he rose to his feet and signalled to his men.

"If we need you further, Miss MacIntosh, you will be here? Jah?"

I nodded, and the Inspector and his team left the room.

Niall followed them. "I feel like something stronger than coffee," he observed. "Coming?"

I shook my head. I did not feel like facing the curious crowd which would be assembled in the bar parlour. News of the Inspector's interest in me would be known all over the place by this time, and I could imagine the barrage of questions I might have to face.

"I think I'll go up and lie down for a while."

Niall shrugged. "Very well. How about you, Crispin?"

"I have some notes to finish. I shall join you later."

"Right." Niall left the room.

I stood up, but instead of going out into the hall and upstairs to my room, I crossed to the window of the sitting-room and stared out across the rippling Austrian meadow, with its mille fleurs pattern of colourful Alpine plants, at the lowering mass of the Schwarzberg away to the right.

Yesteryear, I had thought the mountain, after which the Inn and village in its shadow had been named, had had a friendly, protective quality. Today, it seemed to loom menacingly, like a threat of doom, as its shadow encroached on the sunlit scene.

I shivered at the thought and turned away.

"You are not going to leave the Schwarzberghof with a happy heart, are you, my poor Miranda?"

Jon Crispin had put away his notebook and was watching me critically.

"I shall never come back," I replied slowly.

"And perhaps in time, today's events will fade from my mind, and I will remember only the sunshine, and the flowers, and the mountain music, and the happiness I once knew here."

"And Liesl and her family? Have you no regrets at the ending of a friendship?"

"But our friendship will go on!" I protested. "I shall visit Liesl in Salzburg after she is married. Because I don't want to come back to this particular spot, does not mean I shall not come back to Austria."

"In the meantime, however, Miranda, if you have any sense at all, you should go upstairs, as you told your friend Niall you were going to do, but instead of resting, if I were you, I would pack my bags and hie me for home to Scotland as fast as that little scarlet Sunbeam of yours will take you!"

"Why the urgency, Mr. Crispin?"

"Jon," he smiled in contradiction. "You make me feel too avuncular when you persist in the 'Mr. Crispin' routine." His smile vanished. "But to reply to your question, my dear, I think there is need of urgency in your leaving here.

"Don't you realize, woman," his gaze was stern, "that you are in rather a dangerous situation? You have pointed the finger of murder at two men. Inspector Bauer's probings may discover two men who were seen on the Schwarzberg at the relevant time. You could well be asked, however far fetched the probability might be, to try to identify them from their voices. You might even remember something else about the incident which you have forgotten to tell

the police; some turn of speech, some character-
istic in the speaking voice, which would clinch
your identification! These men might not even
be aware how very little you really know about
them, but they will not be prepared to take a
chance with you, any more than they were
prepared to take a chance with old Hans."

Crispin put his hands on my shoulders and
shook me gently.

"Don't you understand, Miranda? As long as
you remain in Schwarzberg, or Austria, possibly
your life could be in danger!"

As his words sank into my brain, and I realized their full import, a coldness crept over my
body. I moved away from him.

"You are exaggerating!" I tried to deny his
commonsense. "If Inspector Bauer thought I
was in any danger, he would look after me."

"As well as he looked after Hans?"

"I would be doubly careful of strangers! I can
take care of myself!"

I was resolved not to be thought a coward
again, even by instinct! Leaving Schwarzberg
like this, on the spur of the moment, would be a
repetition of my earlier behaviour.

Frightened as Crispin's words had made me
feel, I could not, would not act the caitiff once
again!

"Inspector Bauer told me to stay," I reminded
Crispin of the policeman's words to me as he left
the room. "Even if I wished to follow your suggestion, I very much doubt if I could leave here
without Bauer's say so."

"I'll have a word with the Inspector myself,"

Crispin decided. "I can't really see him wanting another murder on his plate!"

"Stop it!" I said fiercely. "I don't think you care a toss what happens to me! You are only trying out my reactions to your suggestions for use in your writings! You know perfectly well nothing you could say would influence Bauer."

Jon Crispin scowled. "You have an unflattering opinion of me, Miranda. Why?"

Why? I repeated his question to myself. Yes, why did I not trust Jon Crispin? Why did I persistently react so strongly against him? Was it my woman's intuition which told me not to take him at his face value, or was there some other reason for my antagonism to him? Was my mind at conflict with the peculiar physical attraction I felt for him?

"What I think of you is unimportant," I said harshly, annoyed at my own disturbing thoughts.

"All I know is that the police have asked me to stay here. They would not do so if they thought I was in danger. They know that in the Schwarzberghof I am among friends."

"Are you, Miranda?" Jon Crispin shrugged his shoulders. "How do you know who your friends are? Don't forget," he spoke his next words slowly, stressing each one, so that I could not fail to appreciate their import, "whoever stole into Han's Schmidt's quarters during the night, must have been someone familiar with the Inn—someone who knew about the trapdoor from the loft of the byre buildings. Someone who must be very close!"

Chapter Fourteen

"Miranda! Here you are!" Liesl Langheim came bouncing into the sitting-room, where Jon Crispin and I stood staring at each other.

"Mr. Paterson told me you had gone up to your bedroom to lie down, and when I could not find you there, I got quite a shock!"

My friend's arrival broke the numbing spell which Crispin's foreboding words had cast on me.

"I am just on my way upstairs." I took Liesl by the arm and piloted her through the hall, up the stairs, and along the corridor to my room.

I closed the door firmly behind me, told Liesl to sit down, and quickly recounted to her all that had happened during my interview with Inspector Bauer.

The look on her face when I told her that at one point I had actually been charged with the murder of both Rudi Schneider and Hans Schmidt was so comical, I had to laugh, but there was an edge of hysteria to my laughter.

I finished by telling her of Jon Crispin's proposal that I should hot foot it from the Schwarzberghof that very afternoon, or as soon as I could possibly manage to.

Liesl looked at me gravely.

"I thank God for those guests who arrived so late last night," she spoke with feeling. "Had it not been for them, I would have slept in my own bed and not in yours, and heaven knows what

would have happened in that case!" She heaved
a deep sigh.

"For once in my life, I have occasion to be
grateful to my step-father!"

She came over to me and embraced me
warmly. "My poor friend! What a time you have
been through."

I hugged Liesl affectionately in return. It was
wonderful, at such a time, to have with me
someone who cared for me and whom I could
trust.

"You know, my dear," Liesl spoke thoughtfully, "when I consider the advice Herr Crispin
gave you, I find I am in agreement with him."

I looked at her, taken aback.

"Yes, Miranda," she nodded. "The more I
think over what has happened, the more sense I
see in his advice. For my peace of mind, as one
who loves you as well as for your own sake, I
think you should get away from here as quickly
as possible. Come!" she said decisively, bending
down and pulling my suitcase from under the
bed. "I shall help you pack your things."

"Liesl! I can't clear off, just like that!" I protested. "Inspector Bauer wants me on hand in
case he has any more questions."

Liesl snapped her fingers.

"That for the Inspector and all other policemen!"

"You seem awfully anxious to get rid of me!"
I said shakily, as I began to be infected with the
desire to get away with which both Crispin and
Liesl had imbued me.

"I would much rather have a pen friend than

a dead friend!" said Liesl, skilfully folding my skirts and pullovers, and putting them between sheets of polythene in the case.

"What if the Inspector spots me leaving? He would be furious!" I said.

"I don't see how he can keep you here against your will," said Liesl matter-of-factly. "You haven't been charged with anything, officially anyway."

"He could think of something."

"He surely wouldn't stop you going down to Lentasch to visit our friend Trudi—especially if I were with you!"

"The moment he saw the car loaded with cases he would know I was up to something." I sighed. "I don't honestly see how I could sneak away without creating an almighty fuss."

"How about asking Mr. Crispin, or Mr. Paterson, to help?" Liesl was determined I should get away.

"I very much doubt if Niall would approve of my 'moonlight flit'." I shook my head. "He likes things to be done legally and above board! You should have heard how he went on at me this afternoon for not telling him the true story of my adventures right away!"

"Then, it will have to be Mr. Crispin," decided Liesl. "After you and I leave, he could collect your cases and follow us to Lentasch. It's only about twenty or so kilometres from the border. You could be safely in Germany in under half an hour from there, and Mr. Crispin would drive me back here again."

"I couldn't do that!" I protested. "You would both get into trouble."

"I don't see why," said Liesl. "We could say we didn't realize what you were up to. They couldn't prove we were involved." Beaming at her own cleverness, she snapped my case shut.

"I'll carry this one along to Mr. Crispin's room now and go downstairs and enlist his aid. I am sure he will be only too happy to help you!"

"No, Liesl! If I am getting out, I am getting out under my own steam. I will not involve anyone else."

I shoved my slippers into a corner of my second case.

"I hope I have enough petrol in the tank to get me across the border—and talking of borders, Liesl, I gave Herr Katz my passport when I signed in. Be a pet and get it for me now, will you? I can't ask for it myself, in case it might rouse suspicion of my intentions, but you could get it from the desk, couldn't you?"

"It was as well you remembered about it," giggled Liesl nervously. "You would never have got across the frontier without it, and the fact you didn't have it would have caused a lot of awkward questions."

She hurried away, and I locked my cases and checked I had my green card for the car, my travellers' cheques and all other documents I might need readily to hand.

Was I acting wisely or foolishly, running away like this?

Only time would tell.

I looked out, for what I thought would be the last time, on the Schwarzbergthal.

The scent of newly mown hay assailed my nostrils with poignant sweetness. The tall, white marguerites, the purple knapweeds, the deep blue scabious and columbines, the orange mountain dandelions and hawkweeds flaunted their colourful blooms among the high grasses of the undulating slope of the meadow, which stretched from the end of the Inn's patch of garden to the woods above the village; the golden onion of the church glowed with reflected light, and the soft white mists, which invariably settle round the crests of the Schwarzberg in the late afternoon, softened the stark outline of the craggy summit.

I do not think I have ever seen the valley look so beautiful, and there was a tightness in my throat as I turned from the window at Liesl's re-entrance.

My friend looked at me with tragic eyes.

"Miranda! I can't find your passport. It must have been put in the safe, and my step-father has the keys. I dare not ask him for them!"

I sat down on the bed and stared at her blankly.

So that was that.

The reluctant move I had been about to take had been blocked and I was, so to speak, back in square one. Without a passport, I was as much a prisoner in Austria as, short of being behind bars, it was possible to be.

I looked up at Liesl's distressed face.

"It seems you aren't going to get rid of me as

easily as you thought!" I tried to sound much brighter than I felt. "Perhaps this is for the best, after all."

"Miranda!" Liesl flung her arms round my neck. "I am so sorry."

"Don't worry, please!" I pleaded. "Nothing is going to happen to me. Only the good die young!"

"I shan't leave your side for a moment!" she replied fiercely. "I shall be a better watchdog than anyone that Inspector Bauer could choose."

"We had better unpack." I unlocked my cases. "We don't want the police to get the wrong idea, if they should happen to search this room."

Dresses and skirts, underwear and stockings were restored to the drawers and wardrobes far more quickly than they had been removed.

"Mama is coming home tonight," said Liesl as she helped me. "When she heard about Hans, she changed her mind about extending her holiday."

"You will be glad of that," I exclaimed.

"She won't be home until after dinner tonight, so I am still in charge for a few hours." Liesl pushed the emptied cases back under the bed.

"Fortunately, I had prepared most of this evening's meal early and Joseph, for a wonder, has decided to be helpful, so that I can spend more time with you, or so he says! I do not know what has got into him today, unless it is that old Hans' death has worried him."

I had the feeling that young Joseph's con-

science could be troubling him, after the tales he
had told about me to the Inspector, but I held
my tongue. There was enough trouble about,
without stirring up any more unnecessarily.

"If Joseph wants to help, that is all that mat-
ters, not the reason behind it." I patted my hair
into position.

"Come, Liesl, there's no good my feeling sorry
for myself up here, and there is no reason why I
shouldn't be safe in the Inn with all my friends
around me.

"Let's go downstairs and get Heinrich to mix
us up one of his famous concoctions to cheer us
up before you have to leave me to prepare your
final meal as mine hostess, pro tem, of the
Schwarzberghof!"

Chapter Fifteen

My arrival in the bar parlour was greeted with a second of surprised silence, which was followed by a minor uproar as everyone asked me questions at the same time, about why Inspector Bauer had wanted to see me, and if it was true I knew who had killed Rudi Schneider.

Even Irma Werner lost some of her coolness of manner as she eagerly asked if it was true that there had been an attempt on my life as well!

It was obvious that the wildest of rumours had been going the rounds, and my head started to ache as question after prying question was fired at me.

Niall Paterson nobly came to my rescue.

"I am acting for Miss MacIntosh in this matter," he replied in his flawless German. "She has nothing to say to you. She has been told by the police not to discuss the affair with anyone."

I smiled at him gratefully, but I was not to get off as easily as I hoped.

A group of reporters who had come up from Innsbruck, when the news of the murders had broken there, kept plying me with questions. I kept replying, like a robot, that I had nothing to say. I repeated the words so often that I finally convinced them I meant what I said, and they drifted from the bar to find someone with a knowledge of the case, who would be more co-operative with them.

I breathed a sigh of relief when the last

newsman took his departure, and sat down with Liesl at a table near the bar counter.

Niall sat down beside us.

"We've got rid of the vultures meantime, Miranda, but I'm afraid you will not be able to escape their questioning for ever. If you have any sense, you should keep out of sight as much as possible."

He asked us what we wanted to drink and Liesl suggested "Heinrich Specials".

While the barman was mixing the concoction, Joseph came in, looked round and, spotting Niall, came over to tell him there was a long distance call for him, which he could take in the private office.

Knowing what some long distance calls can be like at Schwarzberg, I suspected he would be away for quite some time!

No sooner had he left than Jon Crispin, who had been scowling at me from his perch on one of the high stools at the bar counter from the moment I had come into the room, eased himself to the ground and came over to our table.

"So you did not think my advice worth taking, Miranda MacIntosh?" He shook his head, laid his glass of beer on our table, and sat down beside us.

I looked hastily round to see who was within earshot, before answering in a low voice:

"Liesl backed you up, when I told her about your suggestion. She even persuaded me to adopt it!"

"Good girl!" The scowl vanished from Crispin's saturnine face. "When do you plan to leave? After dinner? I should not leave it too late, if I were you. Your getaway will be safer and simpler at an hour when the roads to the frontier are still busy."

"I said I fell in with your suggestion—"

"After a great deal of persuading," interjected Liesl softly.

"But fate decided otherwise!" I ended, ignoring the interruption.

"What do you mean? What has happened since I last saw you?" demanded Jon sharply.

"The small matter of a passport cropped up!"

"I don't understand—surely, your passport is in order!"

"My passport is in order all right," I sighed. "It also happens to be in Herr Katz's safe, secure under lock and key!"

Crispin swore under his breath.

"Liesl, couldn't you get it for her?" he demanded.

"My step-father never allows the safe key to leave his possession. I would have to ask him to get the passport, and he might wonder why Miranda should need it at this time of night."

"That does make things awkward," he agreed. "Unless," he stopped short as Niall returned to the table.

"Friends of mine want me to visit them in Munich tomorrow," he told us. "It's a bit of a nuisance, but they are clients of mine, as well as friends, so I did not want to turn down the invitation."

Crispin's foot touched mine under the table.

"Why not take Miranda with you for the

day?" he suggested. "It would do her good to get away from the police and the reporters, don't you think?"

Niall's eyes gleamed.

"I didn't think of that! What a good idea! What do you think of it, Miranda?"

"I think it is a wonderful idea!" I breathed with relief.

Here was my way out. Now I had a good excuse to approach Herr Katz and ask him to return my passport, since I would require it to go to the Bavarian capital with Niall.

Niall offered Crispin a cigarette and, as he struck a match to light it, his eyes looked speculatively at the other man.

"Don't you think Miranda should go even further than Munich?" he propounded cautiously.

"Legally, what I am thinking is wrong, but as a friend of Miranda's, it strikes me that the best thing for her is to get away from here as soon as she can."

I expelled a long breath, but Crispin's pressure on my foot increased, as if warning me not to say that we had worked this out already.

"What would Bauer say?"

"I daresay he would be annoyed, but what could he do if you were safely in your own country? And believe me, Miranda," he took my hand in his in a possessive way which made me flush, "it is your safety, my dear, which interests me. We would all be fools if we didn't appreciate that you are not safe here in Schwarzberg, whatever precautions Bauer may take.

"He took precautions with Hans, and we all

know what happened to him!" Niall's lips tightened grimly. "I want you to stay alive, Miranda." He pressed my fingers.

"We all want Miranda to stay alive," Crispin said tartly. "I agree with you she would be safer out of the country."

"You had better not pack your things, or do anything at all which would rouse suspicion," decided Niall firmly. "Liesl can send them on to you later."

"How about my car?" I thought suddenly.

"The A.A. might be able to do something about recovering it for you. Failing that, I am quite sure someone would be willing to bring it home. Still, for the moment, that is not an important issue."

Niall looked pleased with himself. "Now that your safety has been taken care of, Miranda, I feel much happier. How about a toast to a pleasant journey?"

He beckoned Heinrich to bring another round of drinks, but this time, Liesl and I opted for a 'Soda mit Himbeer,' instead of the barman's stronger concoction.

"Gute Fahrt!"

The other three raised their glasses to me, wishing me the traditional German "Pleasant journey".

I smiled my thanks.

We talked of Niall's quickest route to Munich, and he decided to go by Garmisch-Partenkirchen. If we had been touring, he would have preferred the slower and more picturesque route past Walchensee, the deepest and perhaps the best known mountain lake in Bavaria, since he had never visited the region before, but for my sake, he thought we should get to Munich as quickly as possible, where he would see me safely on a 'plane for home.

"Niall! Don't let me spoil your plans," I protested. "So long as I am out of Austria, there surely isn't all that need to hustle me home. If we left fairly early, you could still go by the route you originally planned."

Niall shook his head.

"I can do my sightseeing later," he said firmly.

"You will find plenty to see," I smiled. "Remember, Liesl, the summer your father took us on a tour of what he described as Ludwig's Castles?"

"I could have done with the dinner table at Schloss Linderhof last night!" smiled Liesl.

Crispin looked interested.

"What is so special about that particular table?"

"Have you never heard about it?" I was surprised. "You know how Ludwig the second of Bavaria was for ever constructing fairy-tale castles all round his countryside? Well, this one at Linderhof is, I think, the most elaborate. They say even in those days there were staff problems, so this famous dinner table was constructed in such a way that it could disappear into the floor from the dining-room to the kitchen below, and re-emerge completely set up for a meal!"

"It was a pity the Emperor didn't think of using his talents in other directions," said Niall. "Instead of squandering the country's money on a lot of useless buildings, he could have spent it on more useful ends and made Bavaria a leading nation."

"I think poor Ludwig was looking for happiness, not power," Liesl surmised. "And I know for myself, I should rather be happy, than powerful."

"You are a woman," Crispin entered the argument. "Some men prefer power to happiness, or perhaps the feeling of authority gives them happiness of a kind."

"I am a woman, and I almost forgot my place is in the kitchen!" giggled Liesl. "I didn't realize it was so late. I hope I shall be able to serve dinner on time!"

Chapter Sixteen

I finished my glass of himbeer juice and stood up.

"Niall—Jon," I looked at my two companions, "if you will excuse me, I think I shall go up to my bedroom for a rest before dinner." I frowned with pain. "I have a raging headache developing."

"That is not to be wondered at!" said Niall sympathetically. "You have had quite an exhausting day, Miranda."

"And it all started out so well!" I sighed, touching the pendant Niall had bought for me in Innsbruck.

"Do you have any aspirins?" he asked.

"Their equivalent," I assured him, checking in my handbag to make sure the pills were there.

As I did so, a mob of noisy students from the camping site outside the village came surging into the bar parlour. In seconds, every available stool and chair was occupied.

Heinrich, the barman, who had come over to clear the glasses from our table and see if we wished to order another round, looked none too pleased as the chattering youngsters took over the place.

One young lad, with the face of an angel and the cheek of a devil, whistled for the attention of the bartender.

Heinrich ignored him, but I didn't.

I snapped my fingers.

"That reminds me of something I completely forgot to mention to Inspector Bauer!" I gasped.

Jon Crispin looked at me sharply.

"What was it that you forgot to mention? Something that will be of help in his inquiries?"

I started to shake my head in denial, but pain stopped the gesture short.

"I don't think so," I said, screwing up my eyes against the pounding ache. "However, he did tell me that if I remembered anything, however trifling it might seem, about yesterday afternoon's incident, I was to let him know."

"You were so sure you had told him everything," Niall frowned. "What reminded you of this particular thing you forgot to tell him?"

"It was that lad at the counter and his whistle," I began my explanation. "I know what I have to tell the Inspector is probably of no use to him at all, but when these two men strode past my hiding place yesterday, one of them was whistling."

Niall laughed.

"I wouldn't say that particular piece of information will be of much use to Inspector Bauer!"

"I don't suppose so," I agreed. "Still, I had better mention it, don't you think?"

I passed a hand over my eyes, which were blurring with the pain of my headache.

"I'll say this much, the man was not much of a whistler! I could not identify the tune he was attempting, although it is one I am sure I should know."

"All   popular   music   sounds   the   same

nowadays," Niall scoffed. "Most of it is quite tuneless. I am not surprised you could not identify it, for even I can hardly tell one modern melody from another."

"This was not a pop tune," I denied, pursing my lips thoughtfully. "Nor was it a tune I know very well. It reminded me of the sort of beer garden music you hear in the taverns here. You know the kind of thing I mean. Yet it wasn't that either! I wish I could remember where I have heard it before. It was in connection with something, I feel sure. Damn!" I sighed. "Now that it has come back to mind, I shall be awake all night trying to remember what it is called!"

"Couldn't you hum it for us?" suggested Crispin. "One of us might recognize it."

"You certainly wouldn't, if I hummed it!" I replied. "I love music. I enjoy playing the piano, but when it comes to singing, I am a dead loss, as even my best friends would tell you!"

"I doubt if Inspector Bauer will attach much importance to this fresh news item," Niall shrugged. "I don't see how it could help him, do you? But the reporters would no doubt make something of it. You know how they like a dramatic headline—'The Musical Murderer' sort of thing."

"This murderer's whistle was far from musical," I said. "His whistle was the most tuneless thing I've heard for a long time."

By this time, the students were creating such a cheerful din, I was almost shouting to make myself heard, and my head, was pounding, so that I felt sick.

"I must get away from here!" I said frantically. "Listen, if either of you should happen to see Inspector Bauer, tell him what I have told you, will you?"

Heinrich, who had wiped the damp rings from our table, and was patiently waiting to see if Jon or Niall wished any more to drink, excused himself for interrupting our conversation.

"Bitte. Another beer, Herr Paterson? Herr Crispin?"

Both men shook their heads and stood up to follow me from the room.

"I am going to check my battery, tyres and so on in preparation for our trip to Munich tomorrow, Miranda," Niall said softly. "That way we shall waste no time in the morning."

"Are you sure a cool walk down to the village wouldn't do your head more good than a couple of aspirins?" asked Crispin. "I always enjoy a walk before dinner."

"No, thank you, Jon." I halted at the foot of the stairs. "I am going to try and get an hour's sleep, so if you should see Bauer, tell him I am tucked up safe and snug in my bedroom until dinner time, and I would prefer if he didn't disturb me until later."

"I trust your headache will have vanished before the supper gong goes," said Jon, "and I'll tell Liesl to see that you are left in peace for the next hour."

I went upstairs to my bedroom and locked the door behind me.

By this time my headache was of the blinding variety and I could hardly see across the room.

Wincing involuntarily with the pain of the effort, I pulled off my jersey, stepped out of my tartan skirt, took off the pendant Niall had given me and placed it on my dressing table, before swallowing a couple of pain killing pills and lying down on the bed.

I closed my eyes and hoped for sleep, but sleep would not come for I kept hearing, over and over again, the flat whistling of the man on the Schwarzberg, but try as I might, I could not put a name to the tune.

I opened my eyes and stared across the room out of the unshuttered window.

Night had fallen and the branches of the pear tree framed a sky, dark as the heart of a purple pansy, in which the lights of distant stars glowed faintly.

Although my bedroom was not directly above the bar parlour, I could hear a muted buzz of voices and the clink of glasses through my open window, and the night breeze, which set the pear tree dancing and brushing its leaves against the window pane, brought the sweet, damp evening smell of the meadow and the ripe fruit in the orchard to my nostrils.

Gradually the monotonous buzz of sound from the bar, the gentle crooning of the wind round the eaves, and the soft rustle of leaves on the glass, lulled me to a contented drowsiness, a peaceful relaxation of the mind which was not sleep, but very near to it.

I could hear my own deep, even breathing above the noises which filtered into my room from outside, and I knew I was hovering on the precipice of slumber, when a scratching noise, differing in quality from the scraping of the branches on the wall outside, alerted my senses and made me feel uneasy, utterly breaking the drowsy spell of lassitude.

I continued to breathe deeply as I waited for the sound to be repeated, and when it was, I recognized it for the creak of the rocking chair by my window.

Yet why should the chair creak unless someone was on it, or had inadvertently knocked against it?

The feather touch of fear tickled my spine, so that I shivered under the light weight of the feather plumeau.

Someone must be in my room!

But how could they be? The door was locked.

My eyes glimmered open. I could not see the starlit sky through the window. The scene was blotted out by a dark shape moving swiftly, silently towards me.

As I pushed the plumeau away and struggled to sit up, the black shape pounced.

I had one quick impression of a queerly distorted face and then fingers, strong as steel, grabbed me by the throat. I tried to scream, but these awful fingers choked out sound.

I wasted a precious second trying to prise loose the fearful stranglehold before I remembered the instructions I had been given by an old policeman, who did not approve of women gadding about on their own, unless they knew how to look after themselves.

"Never try to defend your honour, fight for

it!" he had advised me. "Defence is never any good. You must counteract. Take the other fellow off balance!"

As my assailant's fingers tried to choke the life out of me, I called on all my reserves of courage and, instead of pulling helplessly at the throttling hands, I lifted my own hand and, with a vicious jab, pushed my long-nailed fingers cruelly up my attacker's nostrils, piercing the gauzy substance which appeared to cover his face, and with my remaining angry strength, sadistically twisted his nose!

He gave a yelp of pain and released his grip, as he in turn tried to tear away my torturing fingers.

I started to scream and scream. There is nothing like a really hearty screech to scare off an attacker, and my yells must have been heard as far away as the village itself.

The man, realizing that any moment now help would arrive, made one last desperate lunge at my throat, but I evaded him, shoved him off balance, and before he could get to his feet, I had unlocked the door and was running, screaming still, down the passageway.

The Werners came dashing from their bedroom and a policeman came bounding up the stairs.

"What's going on?" he stammered.

"There was a man in my room! He tried to kill me!"

I stood in the middle of the corridor, breathing hard, my hand covering my throat where the cruel fingers had been clutching, oblivious to the

fact that I was wearing a very brief white mini-
slip and very little else.

The policeman swore under his breath and
ran along to my bedroom.

Irma Werner, who had been looking at me
with raised eyebrows as if I was telling a tall
story which was much too way out to be be-
lieved, tried to shoo her husband, who was staring at me with too much interest, back to their
room.

A smile touched my lips at her action, as I
wearily withdrew my hand from my throat.

"Mein Gott!" The expression on Irma's face
changed dramatically—for once I saw beyond
the supercilious, sophisticated pose to the real
woman.

"Your throat!" her eyes rounded. "My dear! I
am sorry! I did not realize!"

She came to me and put her arm round my
waist. "Come!" she led me into her own room
and wrapped her own housecoat round me. "Sit
there, my poor child," she swept a pile of clothes
from the bedroom chair.

"Johan!" she turned to her husband, who was
standing irresolutely in the doorway. "Soak
some of the linen towels, quickly!" she ordered.
"Then go for Liesl."

Werner obeyed like a lamb.

Irma wrung out the towels and wrapped them
round my neck.

"That should help." She smiled, and then, her
curiosity getting the better of her, she asked:

"Who was it who did this to you, my dear?"

"I don't know." I pressed the cool towel

against my throbbing neck. "I was asleep, or almost so, when the man pounced on me." I closed my eyes to visualize the scene. "My room was in darkness. All I could see was a black shape, and then, when he was bending over me, an awful, flat-looking face."

"It must have been a sneak thief!" decided Irma. "No one is safe anywhere these days!"

She wrapped a freshly soaked towel round my neck and dipped the first one back in the basin.

I could hear a lot of movement in the corridor outside, and excited voices. Someone rapped on the door, and when Irma called to come in, Inspector Bauer entered, followed by the policeman who had gone to search my room.

"Miss MacIntosh, what happened?" asked Bauer, his face grim. "Decker tells me you were attacked in your bedroom."

"She certainly was!" said Irma angrily. "Look!" She removed the cold compress she had wrapped round my throat, to reveal the ugly weals left on my skin by my assailant's stranglehold.

Bauer's eyes narrowed. "You were very lucky, Fräulein, to escape from this monster." He bent down to examine the bruise marks more carefully. "Very lucky!"

He straightened up. "Do you think you could tell me exactly what happened, Miss MacIntosh?" He signalled Irma to leave the room, but I stopped her.

"It is not fair to put Frau Werner out of her own room, Inspector," I protested. "She and her husband were getting dressed for dinner when

they came to my assistance. I think we should
not disturb them further. I shall answer your
questions in my own room."

I stood up. My throat ached, otherwise I felt
all right.

"Frau Werner," I looked at Irma, "I am very
grateful to you. You have been very kind."

"I was glad to help, Fräulein," she said simply. "I hope you will not suffer too much discomfort."

"Your treatment helped greatly," I said.
"Thank you."

Wrapping the housecoat she had covered me
with more securely round me, I went along to
my own room, followed by the Inspector.

There were two other policemen in the room,
closely examining the window and, presumably,
searching for fingerprints.

"Decker says your assailant jumped from the
window as he arrived in the room," Bauer told
me. "He caught on the branch of the tree out
there, wriggled to the ground and got away in
the darkness."

"I think he came in that way, too," I said, and
told Bauer the events of the previous half hour.
The incident was so fresh in my mind, I am
quite sure I did not miss out a single detail.

Bauer interrupted me twice only.

Once was to say that the distorted look of my
attacker's face was probably given by the fact
he would be wearing a nylon stocking over it for
disguise.

The second time was to commend me for the
manner in which I had fought off my attacker.

"That was quick thinking, Fräulein," he congratulated me.

"It was a lesson I was taught by one of your British colleagues!" I told him.

Once I had finished my story, Bauer went over it, point by point.

"I wish to be quite sure, Fräulein, that you have not overlooked anything, as you did in the story you told me earlier this afternoon, of the events on the Schwarzberg."

"Oh! I had forgotten all about that! Did Mr. Paterson tell you? About the man whistling, I mean?"

"It was Herr Crispin who spoke to me," said Bauer.

"I don't suppose this addition to my evidence is of much use to you, is it?"

Bauer shrugged. "In my job one never knows what might prove useful."

He stood up and looked down at me gravely.

"One thing is plainly evident to me, Fräulein. These men you heard, whoever they may be, have learned of the story you told me, and consequently know you were on hand when they got rid of Schneider.

"They will take no more chances with you than they did with old Hans." His voice was grim.

"You must be aware, Fräulein, that the attack on you this evening is connected with the Schneider murder!"

I stared at him sombrely.

"I am not a fool, Inspector," I spoke in a low voice. "I realized that."

I looked at him, pleadingly. "Don't you think it would be a good idea for me to return home to Britain, as soon as possible? It would give you less to worry about if I was out of the way."

"No!" said Bauer sharply. "You must stay here! I want you to be available, if the need arises, to identify these men by their voices. You need have no further fear for yourself, Miss Mac-Intosh. I shall take every precaution to see you are kept out of harm's way."

"You did not do so well tonight, did you?" I asked bitterly, fingering my bruised throat.

"I was not expecting an attack on you quite so soon," said Bauer harshly. "I did not realize news of your story would travel so fast." He walked to the window and peered out into the darkness.

"Tonight, and every night that you remain here, there will be men on watch beneath your window and at your door. During the day, you will not be permitted to go anywhere without a guard."

"You cannot keep me a prisoner like that!" I protested, thinking of my plan to escape with Niall on the morrow to Munich. "I haven't done anything wrong!"

"I do not intend to keep you under lock and key," denied the Inspector. "You will be free to go wherever you like, as long as you inform me of your intentions. Then I can arrange with one of my men, or even," he smiled kindly, "one of your men friends, to accompany you and keep watch over you."

I lowered my eyes so that he could not see my look of relief.

Niall Paterson, lawyer, would no doubt be regarded by Bauer as an eminently suitable escort!

He would think nothing of me going off with Niall for a drive next morning, provided, of course, he did not learn of Niall's intended destination!

Chapter Seventeen

The Inspector left the room, after ordering his men to close both the windows and the shutters, and make quite sure of their security. When they had done this, the men followed Bauer down the corridor.

I locked the door and went to sit down on the dressing stool. I examined my face in the mirror. My cheeks were pale, my eyes seemed enormous and on the lightly tanned skin of my throat, the impression of my attacker's fingers stood out in angry scarlet weals.

Looking as I did, I did not feel I wanted to show face for dinner among a crowd of curious strangers. I would order dinner in my room and spend the rest of the evening up here on my own.

I picked up the pendant Niall had given me from the dressing table. It hadn't proved much of a lucky talisman!

There was a knock on the door.

I started nervously. "Who is it?" I called.

"Liesl! Herr Werner said you needed me."

"Liesl!" I opened the door. "Did you hear what happened?"

She nodded. "Miranda! Why should all these horrible things happen here?" she asked unhappily. "Thank goodness, Mama will be home after dinner! I never want to be alone in this place again! I wish I had married Franz in the spring as we originally planned, then neither you nor I would be here at this moment."

She twisted her dirndl skirt nervously with her hands.

"Is there anything I can do for you just now, Miranda?" she went on. "I haven't much time to spare, because I am due to serve dinner in ten minutes, and Rosa and her sister have walked out on me, terrified because of what happened! Even my step-father is not available, though I doubt if he would have lowered himself by helping to serve. He has gone to Innsbruck to meet Mama. And, Miranda, there are so many guests for supper tonight I don't know how I shall cope with only Joseph's help."

I banished the idea of asking Liesl to serve my meal in my room. That would have been the last straw!

"Why not close the bar and ask Heinrich and his young assistant to wait at table?" I suggested. "I am sure, under the circumstances, they would be only too pleased to help out."

"I never thought of that!" Liesl beamed with relief. "Miranda, you are smart! Here I come to see if I can help you, and you do the helping!"

"There's nothing you can do for me," I told her, "except to see that I am served with nothing at dinner which requires much chewing!" I gingerly touched my throat. "And here," I stood up and took off Irma's housecoat, "would you return this to Mrs. Werner for me?"

Liesl departed and once more I cautiously locked my bedroom door.

I would have to make an appearance in the dining-room after all, but, I determined, I would not appear looking like death warmed up!

I washed quickly, and from the wardrobe I took out the one really sophisticated dress I had taken to Europe with me. It was of shot silk and its colours were the shimmering blues and greens of the peacock's feathers.

I pulled it over my head and smoothed it down over my hips, before pulling up the long zip at the back.

I stood back to look at myself in the mirror. The garment made me look model-girl slim and, what was more important, its high, mandarin neckline successfully concealed the disfiguring marks at my throat.

Once more I sat down on the dressing stool and very carefully set to work applying my cosmetics. I hid the pallor of my cheeks under a coating of peach-coloured liquid make-up and a dusting of a deeper tone of powder. I took particular care with my eye make-up, applied a pale rose pink stick to my lips, and sat back to study the effect.

It wasn't bad. Not bad at all. At least, I no longer looked like a scared waif!

As a final touch of sophistication, I screwed into my ears a pair of long, dangling, sequin adorned ear-rings, which exactly matched my dress, and which made my eyes seem a deeper green than they were.

I stood up and crossed to the door. My legs felt a bit shaky and I felt the hollow feeling in my stomach I used to get before an important exam.

I drew a long, deep breath to steady my nerves, and then, feeling like an actress making her stage entrance, I walked slowly along the corridor, down the stairs, and into the dining-room.

At my appearance, the babble of conversation stopped short, and every eye in the room was directed on me.

"Bravo!" whispered Irma Werner with a friendly smile, as I passed her table. "You look wonderful! I applaud your spirit."

I smiled at her warmly. "Thank you."

Johan Werner's eyes followed me every inch of the way to my table, but for once he was not checked for his interest in another woman.

To my surprise, both Niall and Jon were seated at my table. They rose as I approached.

"Liesl thought it would be a good idea if you had company tonight." Niall's eyes admired me as he held out the chair for me to be seated.

Crispin's eyes were on my throat, rather than my face, but it was Niall who posed the question.

"How are you feeling now?" he asked brusquely. "Bauer said you had a very narrow escape this evening."

"I don't expect Miranda wishes to be reminded of that!" Crispin reproved him as he sat down on the seat alongside mine.

"I most certainly do not!" I agreed. "Tonight, I would much rather talk of ships and sealing wax, or anything else at all, rather than of what happened up in my bedroom an hour ago."

My voice finished on a wobbly note, betraying the fact that I was feeling a lot less brave than I was making myself out to be, and out of sight, under the table, my trembling fingers played

nervously with the white linen serviette on my
knee.

Liesl's brother Joseph, dressed in a white
waiter's jacket a couple of sizes too big for him,
served me with a plate of soup.

I thanked him, telling him how grateful Liesl
must be for his help, and doing my best to ig-
nore the way his eyes riveted on my neck.

Jon Crispin, noticing the direction of his gaze,
sent the lad off to fetch some bread for me, while
Niall, oblivious to my growing nervousness, plac-
idly resumed supping his soup.

I couldn't start my meal. My hands were so
shaky, I was sure I would spill the hot liquid if I
attempted to spoon it to my mouth, so I sat
there, forlornly staring at the steam rising from
the "Bouillon mit Ei" in front of me, and tried to
pull myself together.

Unexpectedly, under cover of the table, a firm
hand closed over my trembling ones, steadying
them.

"Liesl's soup is always piping hot, isn't it?"
Jon Crispin found an excuse for my hesitation.
"I find I always have to leave it for a minute or
two to cool down."

He gave my hands a final reassuring squeeze,
as Joseph returned with the bread basket and
proffered it to me.

Now I was able to help myself without the
faintest tremor of my fingers, and I smiled my
gratitude to Jon across the extended bread basket.

I had little difficulty in swallowing the soup,
but it was a different matter with the braised

veal which followed. It took me an annoyingly long time to finish this course, because the smallest lump of meat felt the size of a cannon ball as it passed over my throat!

The other diners had finished their meal and left the room by the time we were served with a sweet, but I did enjoy the cool, soothing ice-cream which Liesl sent in specially for my final course.

When we went to sit in the lounge, Crispin ordered an iced coffee for me, considered that it would be easier on my throat than the scalding black coffee I usually enjoyed after dinner. He was a surprising man, I thought, not nearly such a tough person as he made himself out to be.

As we sat in the lounge, Niall on the sofa beside me and Crispin in a stiff-backed chair facing us, Niall took out a packet of cigarettes and proffered them to Crispin.

"I managed to check everything in readiness for our trip tomorrow, Miranda," he spoke softly, after looking round quickly to make quite sure no one could eavesdrop on our conversation. "I even have enough petrol in the tank to take us across the border to Mittenwald. We can fill up there."

"Niall! Are you still sure you do not mind taking me with you?" I asked. "It is only fair to tell you that less than an hour ago, Inspector Bauer informed me that he wanted me to stay on here, in case I am needed as a witness at an identity parade."

"What help would you be at an identity parade!" scorned Niall. "You never saw the fellows, did you?"

"I heard them," I reminded him.

"A lot of help that could be!" he snorted. "Moreover, how long does he expect you to hang around? He might never catch the scum for weeks, months even, if ever!" His voice rose angrily. "His attitude is preposterous!"

"Sssh!" warned Jon Crispin, as Niall's enraged voice drew curious glances to our little group.

Niall took a long draw at his cigarette.

"Bauer is playing with Miranda's life," remonstrated the lawyer in a lower tone. "We know what happened this afternoon! Miranda is lucky to be alive!" he whispered fiercely. "No! Whatever the repercussions for me, my dear," he assured me, "I am going to take you across the German frontier tomorrow morning, and I will not leave your side until you step on to the London 'plane at Munich airport."

"Niall! You are taking far too big a risk for a stranger."

"For a stranger!" he echoed, staring at me. "Surely, by this time, you don't think of me as a stranger, Miranda!" The look in his eye made me flush. "To me you—but no matter," he stopped hurriedly. "The important thing for the meantime is to get you safely home first and worry about what Bauer will say to me later. Don't you agree, Crispin?"

"I agree with Miranda about the risk you are taking," Jon said slowly. "Of course, the decision is yours, and I take it that as a lawyer you have weighed up the pros and cons of the matter with care."

"Naturally," confirmed Niall.

"You realize that this action could affect your career?" Jon nagged on.

"Yes!" said Niall, "but do you think there is a man or woman in England who would disagree with my decision?" He sounded almost smug.

Jon looked at him critically.

"You *have* considered all the angles, haven't you?" he said thoughtfully. "You are a smart fellow, Paterson."

Niall smiled at the compliment, but I thought Jon's words were two edged. To my ears, he did not sound as if he admired Niall's brand of smartness.

Jon caught me looking at him, and whether he guessed what I was thinking or not, I could not tell, as he blandly turned his attention to me and asked:

"Have you asked Katz for your passport yet, Miranda?"

"No," I shook my head. "Katz has gone off to Innsbruck to meet his wife and bring her home. I shall have to wait until he gets back."

"Let's hope he returns at a reasonable time," frowned Niall. "It would look odd if you had to wait up until midnight to ask him."

"I wouldn't need to do that! I can easily ask him to give it to me first thing in the morning, if he comes home too late tonight."

"That would rouse Bauer's suspicions!" snapped Niall, "particularly if he saw you drive off with me toward Germany shortly afterwards."

"Why?" I asked. "All roads from here lead north to begin with. Why should we be heading for Germany? Moreover, if I am carrying no luggage, and my clothes are lying unpacked in the bedroom, why should he suspect I have no intention of coming back?"

"Because of your asking for your passport," snapped Niall.

"What's so strange about wanting my passport? I am short of money. No bank will cash my travellers' cheques unless I also show them my passport. That's all there is to it."

"Clever girl!" chortled Niall in approval. "I never thought of that angle."

"When it comes to trying to save one's own skin, believe me, one thinks of every angle!" I assured him.

"After that attack on me tonight," my fingers touched my throat involuntarily, "I have thought of everything that will help to get me away from this place!"

Chapter Eighteen

The Werners came over to us and asked if they could join us.

My first impression of the couple, and particularly of Irma, had been proved wrong, as her kindness that afternoon had demonstrated. Now, as we all talked together, with Crispin skilfully asking questions which prompted interesting answers, I learned a great deal about their background.

Irma's parents had both been killed in a wartime raid on Berlin, a fact which possibly accounted for her original antipathetic manner towards me and my friends, and she summed up her feelings later in the conversation when she shrewdly remarked that while nationals can feel bitterness and distrust of other nationals, individuals can often break down this barrier of animosity, and she agreed with me that with the widening scope for travel of the man in the street, there was more chance of friendship between alien races.

"Nationalists and politicians should be banished for all time," Werner acknowledged. "They foment misery and hatred." He spoke with bitterness.

I wondered at his tone until Irma said:

"Johan speaks from the heart. His mother was a Jewess."

"The past is past," said Niall, and quickly changed the subject. "You are an editor on a

woman's magazine, aren't you, Mrs. Werner?
Your work must be most interesting."

"Interesting, but difficult and trying. One has
to be a bit of a psychologist, a bit of a seer, a bit
of a romantic and a bit of a realist to anticipate
what the public wants to read about from week
to week. There is nothing new under the sun,
you know, and the strain of trying to put over as
original something one knows is old, is sometimes too much for me. The same goes for
Johan. He is a dress designer, did you know? We
often work in collaboration."

"Lucky man!" said Jon Crispin with a grin.
"Fancy spending your working hours among
bevies of beautiful young women! You don't
need an assistant, do you?"

"It is not like that at all," protested Johan. "I
work mostly at my drawing board."

"And I pick the models he uses!" Irma's eyes
glinted.

"You would make a model girl yourself," said
Niall gallantly.

"I was, for a few years," admitted Irma.
"That was how I met Johan."

"You must give me some hints as to what the
future fashions are going to be," said Jon.

I was surprised at his interest, as was Irma.

"It's all right, Mrs. Werner. I don't want to
steal your husband's designs and get on the
market first! The truth is, I have a number of
women to clothe," he paused, looking at me and
twinkling at my shocked expression. "In my
books!" he went on calmly, still looking at me,

and still twinkling at my sudden, shame-faced grin.

"Yes, it isn't easy to keep ahead of fashion when you describe your heroine's clothes, because fashion can change overnight—take the new look, for example—and the girl you dress in what is 'with it' today could appear dowdy on publication date a year hence."

"Négligées don't change all that much," Niall said nastily, but his little dig at the novelist was passed over by Irma Werner, who said in protest:

"But they do! Fashion lingerie changes as much, if not more, than outer wear. Don't you agree, Miss MacIntosh?"

"Come to think of it, I do! Why, even stocking styles change, and as for shoes, you could spend a fortune there keeping up with current fashions."

"Women spend too much time and money on dress," Niall scoffed.

"We do it for your pleasure, Herr Paterson." There was a naughty gleam in Irma Werner's eye.

"Look at your friend, Miss MacIntosh, for example. Now, you must admit you admire the dress she is wearing, which she has obviously chosen with an eye for the cut and colour which will present her at her most attractive!"

I blushed as the other four members of our group eyed me critically.

"I like the ear-rings," said Jon. "They are most provocative! They make your eyes green and wicked looking and challenging! We had a tabby cat once with eyes like that. We had a devil of a time keeping the toms away!"

He kept looking at me in a way which made me feel a strange excitement in my blood, and I had to drag my gaze from him to look at Niall, whose light blue eyes were assessing me more impersonally.

"I must admit I like the dress Miranda is wearing. Particularly the colour. On the other hand, a girl as attractive looking as she is would look charming in anything. I would like to see her in one of the delightful, undated dirndl outfits worn by the women of this district. These dresses are proof of what I have been saying that you do not need changing fashions."

"And I would like to see you, Niall, in a pair of brief lederhosen, with embroidered braces, and a natty Tyrolean hat," I responded sweetly. "Think of the sensation you would cause, walking to the Law Courts!"

At the picture I had conjured up, Jon Crispin flung his head back and let out a loud guffaw of laughter, which made the other people in the long sitting-room turn to look at our corner with smiles on their faces.

Irma giggled like a schoolgirl, and Johan Werner's long face brightened into a grin.

Only Niall was not amused, but I had previously noticed he was not very humorous by nature.

I hoped my retort had not offended him, especially when he was going to put himself out so much for me the next morning.

"Niall," I touched his arm and looked at him

in contrition, "I didn't mean to make fun of you."

"That's all right," he replied stiffly. "I am glad I afforded you all some amusement." But he continued to look peeved, and his attitude cast a blight on our gaiety.

In a few minutes, the Werners excused themselves, saying it was time they went for their usual evening stroll before turning in.

After they had gone, Jon Crispin gave a bored yawn.

"It's stuffy in here, isn't it?" He stood up. "How about following the Werners' example, Miranda, and coming with me for a stroll in the moonlight?"

"I would enjoy that!" I jumped to my feet. "I shall have to go up for my coat."

"You must be out of your minds, the pair of you!" snapped Niall. "Don't you realize the insane risk it would be for Miranda to go out walking at this hour? Anyone could be lurking in the woods."

"I wasn't proposing to take her to the woods," said Jon, his eyebrows raised. "Only for a walk round the Gasthof to give her a breath of fresh air before bedtime."

"Miranda can get all the fresh air she needs when she is safely home in Scotland!" Niall stood up and glared at Jon.

"To hear you, I don't think you have appreciated the danger the girl is in, Crispin, or," his eyes glinted, "don't you care?"

The two men stared at each other like fighting cocks.

I didn't know what to say. If I went with Jon, I would offend Niall, which was the last thing I wanted to do, yet if I refused now to go with the novelist, after my initial acceptance of his invitation, he might think that Niall had the right to order me about, and I did not want Jon Crispin to think that! It was the last thing I wanted him to think.

The timely arrival of Liesl Langheim to tell me that her mother had arrived home, and would like to see me, saved the situation for me. I did not have to decide in favour of either man. My decision was made for me.

"Jon, I would have enjoyed a moonlight stroll, but I'm afraid you will have to excuse me," I told him regretfully.

"I have not seen Liesl's mother for two years and," I lowered my voice, "I do want to have a chat with her before I go away. You understand, don't you?"

At my words, Niall Paterson looked pleased as a man does when he gets his own way.

Jon shrugged his shoulders and said lightly, "That's fate for you! Now I shall have to look round for another pretty girl to flirt with in the moonlight! How about you, Liesl?"

Liesl giggled and shook her head.

"I do not think my Franz would like that!" she told him, but she looked as if she wouldn't have minded going, Franz or no Franz!

It seemed I was not the only female who was attracted, in spite of herself, to this man whose characterization of women in his books showed almost too much knowledge of the opposite sex!

Liesl's mother welcomed me warmly in her private sitting-room. She told me how sorry she had been not to have been at home to greet me on my arrival at the Schwarzberghof, and even sorrier to learn of all the disasters which had overtaken me in the past few days.

"After all these tragedies, Miranda, you will never wish to come back to the Schwarzberghof again," she commented sadly. "But you must, my dear. We should all be unhappy if you did not. You are like one of our family, and next year, with Liesl married and out of the house, the place will seem very lonely to me."

"Perhaps Miranda will be married, too!" said Liesl. "Mama! You should see how much one of our guests, a lawyer from London, admires her! His eyes follow her everywhere, and he gets very jealous when Herr Crispin, the writer I was telling you about, tries to flirt with her."

"Come off it, Liesl!" I laughed. "I met Niall Paterson for the first time three days ago. He is very nice, I admit, but ours is a holiday friendship, no more!"

"With him there is a lot more," protested Liesl. "That is very evident when one thinks how he is willing to take you—"

"You are a born matchmaker, Liesl!" I interrupted my friend quickly, before she could thoughtlessly betray our plan for the following morning. "Even if Mr. Paterson did take me to Innsbruck—" I paused to stress the word, "that does not automatically make him want to marry me."

Liesl, realizing the faux pas she had almost committed, flushed.

"Of course not!" she said quickly. "But there is no doubt at all he is greatly attracted, and you would make a very handsome couple."

"Looks are not everything," said Herr Katz, joining in the conversation for the first time. "A woman should look to a man for guidance and comfort, and a man expects respect and affection from his wife."

He put a hand on his wife's shoulder and Liesl's mother caressed it with her sun-tanned fingers. It was a gesture of intimacy which disturbed Liesl.

"It is time I made the hot chocolate," she said abruptly and hurried from the room.

Her mother looked after her with troubled eyes, and a flash of irritation crossed her step-father's face.

"Don't let Liesl's behaviour upset you, my dear," he said gently to his wife. "Perhaps I have not tried hard enough to make her like me."

"I thought she would have outgrown her resentment of you by this time," sighed Liesl's mother. "She makes no effort to be friendly."

"Girls are daft!" said young Joseph, with sweeping boyish contempt for the opposite sex.

"Don't blame Liesl too much, Frau Lang—Frau Katz," I amended hastily. "As almost one of the family, may I speak?"

Frau Katz nodded.

"It is only natural that Liesl should react as she does. She was her father's favourite and very close to him. She still misses him very much, and she cannot understand how you could marry again."

Katz started to speak, but I shook my head.

"She does not realize how lonely a woman who has been happily married can be, when she is suddenly widowed. I hope she will never have to," I added, "but I believe that when she herself is married, she will learn understanding. As a matter of fact," I assured them, "I feel when her wedding day draws near, she will be relieved that you did remarry, so that when she goes off to Salzburg you will have someone to look after you."

"Liesl is lucky to have a sensible friend like you," said Katz.

"Miranda's not bad for a girl!" agreed Joseph. "She doesn't mind going fishing, or helping me catch lizards and the like." He gave me the highest praise he could bestow!

By the time Liesl returned, conversation was carefully channelled to a discussion of winter skiing in the area, and we spent the rest of the evening pleasantly chatting of old friends and future plans, and sipping strong, hot cups of chocolate.

When finally Herr Katz stood up and said it was time we all retired, I was reluctant to leave the friendly warmth of the family circle.

Liesl had asked her mother's consent to spend another night in my bedroom, although her own room was once again at her disposal. I was delighted about this, since I had been dreading bedtime and the return to the room where I had been attacked. Liesl's chattering presence would exorcize all ghosts!

So we went upstairs together, Liesl clutching a book she had been reading, together with a bag which contained her nightgown.

A man was patrolling the corridor outside my room, and he saluted smartly as we approached, making me feel like a visiting personality!

I felt sorry for the poor man, having to sit up all night for my sake, and when Liesl peeked out between the slats of the wooden window shutters, and told me that there was another man patrolling the orchard below, I appreciated that Inspector Bauer was keeping his promise to keep me as safe as possible.

Tomorrow night, he would be relieved of these precautions, I thought, as I hung my pretty dress away in the wardrobe.

Tomorrow night, I would be safe and snug in my own bed, in my own room, in my own house, in my own native land! Tomorrow night, starting at shadows, sudden fears, and nylon masked murderers would be things of the past!

I sat down at the dressing table to remove my make-up with cleansing lotion.

The paperback book which Liesl had brought up with her lay in front of me, covering the pendant which Niall had bought for me in Innsbruck. It was a book by Jon Crispin.

I picked it up.

On the back cover was a photograph of the author.

It was a good photograph.

It had caught the personality of the man; the

challenge of the dark eyes; the strength of the jawline; the humour that quirked the mouth to a teasing smile; the way the thick, black hair seemed to resent the taming influence of brush and comb.

As I sat there, with the book in my hand, studying the portrait of its author, I had to admit to myself that although I was going to do the wise thing, my foolish heart did not want me to leave Schwarzberg quite so soon, because if I were to be safe in Scotland tomorrow night, I could not be here in Austria to walk in the moonlight with a man who attracted me more than any other man had ever attracted me in my twenty-two years of living!

Chapter Nineteen

My sleep that night was restless. My dreams were a nightmare fantasy, where Jon Crispin was married to Irma Werner and Niall's car could take wings and hop over hay wagons to pass them; where I was being chased up a slippery, steep mountain path by uniformed frontier guards, and Inspector Bauer stood waiting for me at the top of the mountain, laughing at my puny efforts to escape, and laughing with that frightening, chilly, humourless laugh of the man who had murdered Rudi Schneider.

I sat up with a start and hugged myself in fear, thinking the laugh more than fantasy, but as I became fully awake, the laughter no longer filled my ears and I knew it was a dream echo.

Liesl stirred in her sleep, but did not waken. In the moonlight which filtered through the shutter slats, I could see she was smiling. Unlike mine, her dreams must have been happy ones.

I lay down again, pulled the plumeau over my cold shoulders, and I must have dozed off, for when next I opened my eyes the shutters had been pushed back and morning light filled the room.

Liesl was dressed and sitting at the toilet table, brushing her hair. When she saw I was awake, she smiled to me mournfully in the mirror.

"I can't believe that you are going home today, Miranda," she finished pinning up her long

hair. "It makes me feel so sad. Yet I know if it
hadn't been for me, you would not have come
here and, consequently, become involved in this
horrible affair." She turned round to face me.

"You will come back for my wedding, won't
you?"

"Of course!" I assured her. I did not want to
make her more unhappy by adding, "I'll come, if
the Austrian authorities allow me."

After all, if I sneaked over the border today
without telling Bauer my intentions, I might
not be welcome, or even able, to return to Austria.

Liesl crossed to the bed.

"I shall say good-bye to you now, Miranda,"
she said, sighing. "I shall not come out to wave
you farewell when you drive off with Mr. Paterson. It might seem odd if I come out specially to
wish you 'Gute Reise', when you are merely
supposed to be going for a car run."

"Liesl!" I slipped out of bed and hugged my
friend. "Why did everything have to be so different this year?"

She returned my embrace of farewell.

"I hope things will go better for both of us
from now on," I added.

"Ich auch!" said Liesl, with feeling. "Good-
bye, my dear friend. God be with you," and with
tears starting to her eyes, she fled from the
room.

Although it was still very early, I felt too restless to go back to bed and sleep.

I looked out of the window at the bright sunlight and was surprised to see, on the higher

peaks of the Wetterstein Gebirge, that there had been a fresh snowfall, and that this morning the snow line was much lower down the mountains. There was a sharp chill in the morning breeze, which warned me it would be advisable to wear warm clothing for the long journey ahead of me.

I washed, pulled on a pair of olive green ski pants and a thick woollen jumper of the same shade, and stuffed as many of my personal treasures, a nightgown, a change of underclothing and a tricel grey dress, which folded to next to nothing, into the small rucksack I invariably carried with me on my excursions.

Although I was going to have to leave my other belongings at Schwarzberg for the meantime, at least I would have something to change into for my changeover stop in London.

As I checked on the items I was taking with me, I realized that I had forgotten to ask Herr Katz for my passport the previous evening! I had better have a word with him now before anyone else was around.

I hurried downstairs, past the man on duty in the corridor, who showed surprise at seeing me up and about so early, and went in search of Liesl's step-father.

I found him attending to the stove in the breakfast room.

"Grüss Gott!" he greeted me, showing the same mild surprise as the policeman had done at my early appearance.

"I am sorry to trouble you at this early hour, Herr Katz," I smiled, "but I intend to do some shopping today and I shall need my passport to cash my travellers' cheques."

"I am so sorry, Fräulein MacIntosh," he apologized. "I meant to return it to you before this." He wiped his hands. "Come, I shall get it from the office now."

However, it still was not to be my day.

As I stood waiting beside the reception desk, Inspector Bauer appeared and came over to speak to me. I could feel my every muscle tense and the saliva dried in my mouth.

"What are your plans for today, Miss MacIntosh?" he asked, at the very moment at which Katz reappeared, saying:

"Here is your passport, Fräulein!"

"Thank you, Herr Katz." I extended a hand, which only the greatest effort of will prevented from trembling, but Bauer's hand shot out even faster and he seized the document first.

"I think I should take care of your passport for a day or two," he said blandly.

"B-But I need it to get money!" I protested shrilly. "I cannot cash my travellers' cheques without producing my passport."

"I am sure Herr Katz will cash any cheques you need in the meantime." Bauer looked at the innkeeper, who nodded.

And that was that!

I could have argued, but it would have got me nowhere. When Niall Paterson joined me at breakfast half an hour later, I told him the glum news.

He took the setback with a philosophic shrug, and I wondered if perhaps he was rather glad that he wasn't after all going to be involved in an action which would have been frowned on by the authorities.

I gave him a dispirited wave, half an hour later, as he drove off in his sports car for his trip to Munich, and as I walked back to the Inn, feeling completely fed up, I bumped into Jon Crispin.

"Are you sorry because your plan has fallen through, or because you will be without Paterson's company today?" he asked me, his eyes on the Maria-Thérèsa medallion I was wearing, which he knew had been a gift from Niall.

I flushed.

"Why should I miss Niall? He is only a holiday acquaintance, like yourself!"

Crispin shrugged. "From what I have seen, Paterson considers you more than a mere acquaintance. I think he has weighed you in the balance and decided you would fill the bill of the future Mrs. Niall Paterson very well."

"Don't be silly!" I said scornfully. "Niall would never marry someone he met on holiday! As a matter of fact," I smiled, "he told me exactly how he would choose a wife, and he certainly did not pick me that way!"

"What do you mean?" Jon looked interested, so I told him of Niall's theory that there would be fewer marriage failures if people picked their marriage partners by computer.

"The cold-blooded devil!" exclaimed Jon. "I prefer to have my own personal say in my choice of woman! I want someone who is flesh and blood and has the courage to choose her own

man, even if he is the wrong one. I want someone I can argue with. What a deadly bore it
would be," he shook his head, "to live with
someone who agreed with you on everything.
No!" he affirmed, "I would rather a year in hell
with a passionate virago than a lifetime in limbo
with a consenting slave! What do you say,
Miranda?"

I stood for a moment to consider.

"I go along with you, but not all the way. If I
marry, it would be for better or for worse, for
my lifetime."

"Humph," Crispin scuffed the ground with
the toe of his shoe. "So Paterson is no more to
you than a holiday acquaintance," he said
slowly.

I shook my head.

"Good!" said Jon blithely. "In that case, how
about furthering your holidaying acquaintanceship with me? I have to go to Schwach today to check on some copy. Would you like to
come with me?"

I had difficulty in stilling the sudden excited
pumping of my heart.

"Do you think Inspector Bauer would allow
me?"

"Why not? I can take care of you as well as
any of his policemen! I'll go and have a word
with him."

Crispin's 'word' had the desired effect, and
twenty minutes later we were on our way.

Jon's car was a DBS Aston Martin in racing
green. As we sped along the road towards
Innsbruck, I could not help comparing his driv-

ing with that of Niall's. Niall had driven fast,
with a contempt for other road users and a ruth-
lessness which seemed at variance with his character.

Crispin, too, drove quickly, but more steadily,
with fewer sudden surges of speed and sudden
braking. I felt I could relax beside him and enjoy the scenery.

We passed through Innsbruck, keeping to the
left of the river, and half an hour later we
reached our destination. We had morning coffee
in a small, oak-beamed café off the main road,
and then Jon took me to see the famous parish
church with its Gothic tower and enormous cop-
per roof, the two naves, a relic of the old mining
days, one for Catholics, one for Protestants, the
most beautiful bell in Tyrol, and a striking war
memorial.

It was the memorial which particularly interested Jon, and he made several notes about it in
his little book.

We went on to the adjoining graveyard, the
Friedhof or Court of Peace as it is termed in
Austria, and while Jon made more notes in his
book, I wandered down the pathways, noticing
the little bowls of holy water placed at the foot
of each grave, from which numerous little birds
were drinking greedily. I also noted how many
of the men buried here had been killed in the
two great wars. Often a dead soldier's photograph was attached to the small cross over the
grave, and I felt sad to think how many youths
of my own age, with much to live for, had been

wiped out because of the lust for power of psychopathic politicians.

"You would think of all this," I indicated the rows of graves, "and all the other ones to be seen in so many parts of Europe, would teach people the insanity of war."

"My dear Miranda," he shook his head, "the people who start wars do not think of common men. They are obsessed with power and make use of high fallutin' ideologies, like Freitschke's, to excuse themselves."

"Freitschke?"

"The man who said 'peace was a state of sloth" and that the grandeur of war consisted of the 'utter annihilation of puny man in the great conception of the state'!"

"How horrible!" I shivered.

Jon closed his notebook. "Come, my dear, I didn't bring you here to make you miserable. I have checked over what I came for and, if we leave now, we should make Innsbruck in time for lunch."

Chapter Twenty

Over lunch at the "Alt Innsprugge", we talked of travel, and Jon's books and my home, and it was so pleasant to sit and watch his expressive face, and listen to his stories, and even to see how other people in the restaurant took notice of him, that I wanted the lunch break to last for ever.

When the waiter brought the bill, Jon suggested that since we still had the afternoon before us, we should go back to Schwarzberg the long way round by Seefeld.

I was only too happy to agree. The steep, twisting road up to the famous holiday resort could not be traversed at any speed, which meant that not only would I be longer away from any danger which waited me in Schwarzberg, but that I would also enjoy Jon's company for a longer period.

At Seefeld, we turned left on to the Leutasch road, and then left again along the narrow, twisting, gravel surfaced road which branched off to the Schwarzbergthal.

Now we were in a region of towering mountains, and grim grey rocks overhung the route on the left, while on the right there was a sheer drop to the boulder strewn ravine in which one of the tributaries of the Isar foamed and tumbled in an angry torrent. In parts the edges of the track had been washed away by the spring

rains and there were frequent signs warning
drivers to beware of landslides.

Jon drove with great care, since in places the
road was barely broad enough for two vehicles
to pass, and many of the corners of the tortuous
route were blind. Since we were on the outer
edge, there was especial need for him to take
care!

We had reached one of the welcome straight
stretches of the road, when I saw Jon frown as
he glanced in his driving mirror.

"What's wrong?" I asked quickly, turning to
look behind me.

About quarter of a mile away I could see an
open, cream Mercedes sports car.

"I don't like the look of it," said Jon curtly.
"That car has been on our trail since we left
Innsbruck."

"So what?" I shrugged. "This isn't a private
road!"

"Miranda, I don't want to frighten you, but
that particular car also followed us from
Schwach, until I lost it in the traffic in
Innsbruck. I noticed it especially because of the
dent in the grill."

"But why should a car follow us?" I puzzled.

"There are two men in it."

"Police!" I decided. "Bauer has asked his men
to keep an eye on me."

"No!" said Jon sharply. "They aren't police,
Miranda. And I don't think they are following
us for the fun of it!" His foot pressed more
firmly on the accelerator.

"Hold tight, and I'll see if I can leave them—

if not," his lips tightened, "my dear, please do whatever I tell you, without hesitation."

I gave another quick look round.

To my dismay, I saw that the Mercedes was now a mere twenty yards away, and moving out, ready to overtake us.

"They are going to try to pass!" I cried. "They are mad! There isn't room!"

Crispin's foot pressed harder still on the pedal and the car surged forward. We pulled ahead again, but had to brake sharply for another blind corner, and in the next half mile of continuous twists and turns, the cream Mercedes moved a little bit closer, until it was virtually on our tail.

I felt quite sick. Although from the passenger seat I could not see the drop into the ravine, since Jon's car had right hand drive, I had travelled the road several times myself before now, and I knew exactly how deep and how wild the gorge was.

If we were in collision with anything here, we would go over the side like a plummet and never live to tell the tale!

We came to another straight stretch of roadway, a much shorter one than the last, but I expected Jon to accelerate and again gain a short distance, but it seemed as if the power had gone from the car, because it did not pick up speed, and to my horror, the Mercedes went out once more to overtake us. It was now drawing alongside with scarcely a pain breadth between us. Over and above the drumming of the tyres on the grit surface, I heard one of the men in that open Mercedes start to laugh, and my blood ran cold.

This was the same laugh I had heard at the time of Rudi Schneider's murder—it was vicious, wicked and triumphant!

I no longer doubted the intentions of the occupants of that car.

They meant to kill us.

I turned my shocked gaze on them and realized they had got into position to force us off the road. I could plainly see the driver prepare to make the final infinitesimal turn of the wheel which would bring car forcibly against car, and to blot out that awful moment, I closed my eyes.

Jon shouted, "Hold tight, darling!" and before he even finished speaking, my seat belt jerked me painfully alert as with a sudden great surge of power, the Aston Martin leaped forward, tyres raising a scream of protest as we took the fast approaching corner at a speed I would never have dreamed possible.

We made the turn safely, but the Mercedes didn't.

So intent had its driver been on our destruction, he was prepared neither for the acute angle of the bend nor for Jon's sudden burst of acceleration.

Our car was no longer between him and the edge of the ravine to act as bumper for his intentional sideways manoeuvre, and though he struggled like a maniac to correct his steering, he reacted too late.

As if it had been shot from a rocket, the Mercedes went out over the edge of the road.

Jon braked his car to a standstill in the first possible stopping place, and we unfastened our seat belts and went running back along the road.

By the time we reached the scene, the Mercedes was lying at the foot of the ravine, half submerged in the mountain torrent, and its two occupants, who had been ejected from the open car as it somersaulted to its doom, were being tossed like corks on the foaming river and battered against the stony outcrops of the banks, as the current carried them remorselessly through the rapids to the waterfall which cascaded into a gully fifty yards further downstream.

I started to shiver. The horror of what I saw, and the realization that what had happened to the man who laughed as he sent others to their deaths could so easily have happened to Jon and me, made me feel sick and dizzy.

I put my hand up to my eyes, trying to blot out the scene.

"Come, Miranda," Crispin took my arm, "there's nothing we can do, except notify the authorities."

I began to weep.

"Jon! It was awful! It was meant to be us!" I shivered more violently.

Jon's arm went round my waist, holding me close.

I turned and buried my head against his shoulder to weep my fears away, and as I wept, Jon's arms held me comfortingly, one hand stroked my hair gently and soothingly, and all the time he murmured soft words of consolation, until at last I managed to pull myself together and sniff away my final tears of distress.

"I am all right now, Jon," I said chokily. "Sorry to make such a fool of myself." Self-consciously I freed myself from his embrace.

He took a handkerchief from his pocket and wiped the tear stains from my face.

"You were being extremely feminine and natural, my dear." He dabbed away the final damp smudges. "The way I like my women to be," he added, smiling into my still smarting eyes, gently brushing my tousled hair from my forehead and then, to my amazement, kissing me on the mouth with a gesture which started as the light salute of a friend, and then developed into a painful pressure of lips which at first I weakly tried to reject, but which in seconds I succumbed to.

The shrill of the motor horn of an approaching car brought us both smartly back to reality.

"I am sorry about that, Miranda," Jon pushed me roughly away. "This is neither the place nor the occasion for a love scene!" He laughed harshly. "My timing never was good. You must think me an unfeeling brute. Forgive me."

I was too stunned by what had happened to reply.

The approaching car drew near and Jon signalled it to stop. He explained to the driver what had happened, and when he learned that, like ourselves, the man was bound for Schwarzberg, he asked him to contact Inspector Bauer, saying that he himself would wait at the scene of the accident until the police arrived.

At Jon's suggestion, I went on to Schwarzberg with the stranger, and I was glad to do so, not merely because I was still a bit shaken by the accident and wanted to get away from the scene of the tragedy, but also because I was even more shaken by Jon's kiss.

I could not have sat waiting with him in his car, alone, for an hour or more, without revealing to him that although he might consider me merely another pretty woman to flirt with, my own emotions were more deeply involved.

I had my pride, and loving Jon Crispin as I did, I knew I did not wish to be merely another of the many women in his life. I wanted to be the only one, and reading his character from his books, I did not think Jon Crispin was the marrying kind.

The only bright spot of that evening was the fact which emerged from the intense police questioning.

When I told Bauer that one of the men in the Mercedes was one of the men involved in Schneider's murder, since I had immediately recognized his laugh, the Inspector brightened up considerably. It was obvious now that the two men who had killed Hans and Rudi, and also attempted to eliminate me, had gone to their own deaths in their second attempt on my life, which saved him a lot of searching, gave me my freedom, since I no longer needed police protection, and also made Bauer hand me back my passport. As far as I was concerned, the case was over!

Although they could only guess at the motive for Schneider's murder, they felt sure the guide had been killed because of a woman, and there the matter would rest.

When Niall Paterson returned from Munich that evening, it was to find us all celebrating with a champagne party the departure, with the police, of the gloom which had hung over the Schwarzberghof.

We had a very gay evening, in spite of a violent storm which broke overhead during our party, and we ignored the thunder rolls and the torrential rain which flooded down, and the mutterings of the locals in the bar that the downpour would cause further landslides in the hills.

I was glad Niall was back and making a fuss over me, because it meant I could avoid Jon's attentions. I felt self-conscious each time he looked at me, and in an effort to hide my true feelings I took more notice of Niall than I normally would have done.

However, I did make up my mind about one thing. Since I could not possibly keep avoiding Jon Crispin for another week, which was the length of time he proposed to remain at Schwarzberg, I myself would travel back to Scotland on the morrow.

Liesl was most upset when I told her my decision.

"Now that the police have gone and Mama is home again, I should have plenty of time with you, Miranda. Do stay!" she pleaded, but I remained firm.

"At least, wait one more day," she wheedled. "A friend of mine is having her wedding reception here tomorrow afternoon. You have never been to such an affair in Austria, so this will give you some idea what to expect when you come to my own wedding in September!"

I gave in to this demand. Surely, I could avoid being alone with Jon for one day, for avoid being alone with him I must!

Even in a crowded room, one look from Jon could make my bones turn to water! I was glad, this night, of Niall's attentions, and although I did not believe in his computer theory of marriage, I felt that one thing to be said in its favour was that it could not involve one in this hopeless feeling which came from falling in love with the wrong type of man!

I cried myself to sleep that night and woke, for my last full day at the Schwarzberghof, heavy eyed, heavy headed and heavy hearted.

Chapter Twenty-one

It was a bright, sunny morning. I had breakfast early before the other guests were up and about, and told Liesl that I intended to go for a walk up the Schwarzberg to lay the last of my ghosts, and also to see if the pure mountain air would clear my aching head.

Joseph asked if he could come with me.

"Since you won't be coming back to Schwarzberg, Miranda," he said, when his family was out of earshot, "I want to show you a secret!"

He was so eager to come with me, and his family was equally pleased to think he would be out of the way while they coped with the extra preparations for the wedding reception in the afternoon, I could not refuse his request.

Together we set off from the Inn and strolled through the belt of pines to the mountain track. About an hour and a half later, we reached the point from which Schneider had been shoved to death.

I firmly averted my gaze from the fatal spot as we walked past the escarpment and climbed still higher up the mountain, until we came to the point where the track had been abruptly terminated by the great landslide of 1945.

I was hot from the exercise and the heat of the sun, so I begged Joseph to sit down and rest awhile.

He was impatient to keep going, but good manners prevented him persisting in this, so I sat down on a fairly flat slab of rock to enjoy the rest, the soft mountain air on my cheeks, and the warm sun on my back, while Joseph, unable to sit still, aimed bits of scree at the trunk of a lonesome pine tree which stood aloof and straight, pointing its green tip proudly to the sky some thirty feet from where we were sitting.

After a ten minute break, his impatience forced me to rise reluctantly to my feet and continue on our way to his "secret".

The climb was much more difficult now that there was no path to follow, and in actual fact, because of the danger of scree slides and rock falls, Uncle Langheim had warned us all in years gone by against climbing beyond this point. Once or twice Liesl and I had disobeyed the injunction and scrambled a few yards higher up the mountain, but because the going was so steep and slippery and dangerous, and because there was nothing to see but fields and mounds of rubble, with not even a patch of wild flowers to brighten the desolation, even our dream of perhaps seeing our dream castle of Rohrdorf never tempted us too far away from the boundary set by Liesl's father.

"Have we much further to go?" I gasped wearily as Joseph, light-footed as a chamois, climbed the steep slopes in front of me.

"Only another few yards, Miranda!" he called back softly. "Then you will see my secret!"

My clothes were sticky with heat and my nails ragged from hauling myself up the more precipitous stretches by handholds. As for my slacks, they were snagged in a dozen places, and white and powdery from the limey dust of the rocks.

"I shall have to rest again, Joseph!" I groaned. "I am completely out of training for this kind of adventure. Remember, it is two years since you last took me climbing!"

"Girls!" Joseph uttered the word scornfully as he squatted down on a boulder and waited for me.

I was so glad of another rest, I ignored his scorn.

"If we have to be back for 'Mittagessen'," he said impatiently, as I made no further move to go on, "we shall have to waste no more time!"

Once more I scrambled to my feet and followed my eager guide, but I moved with a decided lack of enthusiasm when I saw in what direction Joseph was leading me.

He was walking, very gingerly now, not upward, but along the field of loose scree which had fallen from the topmost peaks of the mountain to a pinnacle of rock which rose up like a needle from the bed of rubble, much as a lighthouse rises above a rocky skerry.

He slithered and slipped as he made his way across the tricky surface until at last he reached the point towards which he had been making, and then with a final spurt of effort, he pulled himself to the top of the tower of rock.

"If this is your wonderful 'secret', Joseph Langheim, you can keep it!" I called angrily. "I am not going to risk my bones for the sake of climbing a shaky rock tower!"

"It's the view you've come to see," he called

back, face alight with excitement. "Come on, Miranda! Come and see this!"

"Joseph! I refuse to move another step! It's too dangerous!"

"I can see something you have always wanted to see," he taunted me. "You'll be wild if you don't come and I tell you later what it is!"

Excitement stirred in my veins. From the top of his pinnacle Joseph must be able to see into that part of Schwarzbergthal which had been blocked by the landslide in '45!

"Come on, Miranda! Hurry! We haven't all day!"

Still I hesitated.

If Joseph could see the lost valley, then he must be able to see the castle Liesl and I had often longed to see, yet now that the moment of revelation had come, now that one of my dreams was to be realized, I felt afraid.

Perhaps if Liesl had been here to share the moment with me I would have gone forward eagerly, or perhaps it was the echo in my head of Jon Crispin's words to me, that dream castles were best left out of reality, which weighed each cautious step I took towards Joseph. Perhaps I felt that I was tempting fate by finding my personal El Dorado. Whatever it was, my reluctant progress made Joseph turn to me with an impatient signal to hurry.

At his movement, part of the rocky pinnacle on which he stood gave way under his feet, and with a startled cry he fell down on to the sloping bed of scree some ten feet below.

His fall set the loose rubble into motion, and

before he could scramble back on to his feet, the shifting scree rolled him on down the slope, like one more stray boulder.

I opened my mouth to yell to him to keep calm, but remembered in time that a sudden loud noise might set up further rock slides, so I did the only thing left for me to do. I went scrambling and slithering after him, and about ten seconds later, expedited by the downward moving rubble, I got alongside him and managed to grab him and haul him to his feet.

The sliding landfall still pulled at our foothold to drag us downhill, but we were able to find an island of solid rock in that sea of waste, and we clambered on to it and sat breathing exhaustedly, unable to speak for a few moments.

In order to reach Joseph, I had had to skirt some twenty yards of mountainside, and the point where we now rested was on that side of the Schwarzberg which I had never attained before, but it was not until I had assured myself that, apart from a few bruises and minor cuts and grazes, and a frightened reaction to his accident which made poor Joseph's teeth chatter like castanets, the lad was otherwise unharmed, that I took a good look at the scene around me.

It was only now that I realized that the ledge on which we were squatting must be a part of the old road over the mountain to Rohrdorf, the road which had been cut off by the landslides and rockfalls of that last winter of the war.

As I looked, I saw something else, which stirred an excited sensation in my veins.

On the left of the ledge, the castle side, there

was a man high cave, which appeared to bore right into the hillside.

Joseph spotted the cave at the same time as I did, and at once the shock of his fall was forgotten, and he was agog with excitement.

"Miranda! Look, a tunnel! Let's see where it leads!"

"No!" I spoke firmly. "We have had enough trouble with your explorer's zeal for one day. What we are going to do now is to try and get back up the scree before it starts moving again. It will take us quite some time and effort!"

"But what if the cave leads out somewhere?" persisted Joseph hopefully.

"Don't be silly! How could it? In any case, it seems to tunnel into the mountain the wrong way for it to be of any use to us."

"Please, Miranda."

"No!" I refused to waver. "On your feet, Joseph, and back the way we came. We can use your look-out rock to guide us."

Joseph looked mutinous. He cast longing glances towards the tempting cave.

"Up!" I said sternly. "You first, Joseph!"

The words were barely uttered when we heard a most unexpected sound coming from the tunnel mouth. Someone inside the cave was whistling.

"Why! There is someone there!" Joseph gasped with excitement: "Miranda! There is someone in the cave!"

Before I could stop him, he darted towards the round, black hole. I was too petrified to call him to a halt.

Yesterday, I had heard a laugh which had boded me no good.

Today, a whistle was my sound of ill-omen, for the tune I heard being whistled at this moment was the tune whistled by the man who had been with the man who had laughed at Schneider's death, and I could not doubt it was being whistled by the same man, because it went off key in the very same places.

"Joseph!" I croaked, finding my voice. "Come back here!"

Joseph came back all right, but not under his own steam. He was being rudely shoved out of the cave by Heinrich, the barman at the Schwarzberghof, and following Heinrich came Niall Paterson!

Niall's face went white as he saw me.

"Miranda!" he gasped. "What are you doing here?"

Before I could answer, Heinrich spat out words in German so vicious and obscene that I quailed back from him.

"We shall have to get rid of them both," he snarled. "Now that they have found the tunnel which leads to Rohrdorf, there is nothing else for it!"

He pushed Joseph roughly towards me and stood glaring at me.

"Once already you almost brought about the discovery of our new leader and our secret headquarters!" his eyes were blazing with rage. "Today, you and this boy, with your curiosity, would do the same again. This time, there is no escape for you!"

He took a step forward and I put my arms round Joseph and glared at our enemy defiantly.

"No, Heinrich! Stop!" Niall spoke sharply. "Kill the boy, but the girl will say nothing—you have my word! I intend to marry her."

I gasped and looked at Paterson in disbelief.

Joseph clung to me in terror.

"They both go over the edge!" Heinrich was remorseless.

I moved swiftly so that my back was to the mountain, away from the edge. Heinrich took another step forward, arms outstretched to seize us.

Joseph let out an eldritch scream of terror; a scream which echoed and re-echoed round the overhanging mountains; a scream which had the same disastrous effects as the trumpets on the walls of Jericho, for even as Heinrich moved within arm's reach the scree above us, loosened by the vibrations of sound, started to move downhill and its sudden surging movement must have brought about the final crack in the base of Joseph's "watch tower".

There was an ear shattering crash, the pinnacle of rock crumbled, and its massive boulders came bowling down over the loose rubble, hurtling straight towards the ledge on which we were all standing.

Heinrich stopped and gaped upwards, but Niall, with quicker apprehension of the danger, sprang towards Joseph and me, and with a hefty shove pushed us both into the tunnel entrance.

As we reached its safety, rocks, scree, boulders

and rubble went thundering past into the valley hundreds of feet below.

Niall, who hadn't quite made the cover of the cave, was struck on the back by an enormous slab of stone and collapsed, face forward, half inside the tunnel, but the lower part of his body, from the waist down, was buried under a mass of debris.

Joseph began to cry, but I whispered angrily to him to keep quiet. One landslide was over. I did not want him to start another as I tried, with frantic effort, to free Niall Paterson from the weight of stone on top of him.

Of Heinrich there was no sign, but the state of the ledge on which he had been standing left no doubt as to his fate.

Niall was unconscious for which fact I was glad, as I slowly eased the rubble from his body and then, as gently as I could, inched him into the cave.

It didn't require much knowledge of first aid to appreciate that if he didn't get medical attention soon, he would die. There was nothing more I could do for him myself, except try to get help.

At this stage, I was beyond thinking of how Niall had come to be where he was: what his connection with Heinrich was, or how he had been mixed up with the murder on the Schwarzberg. All I could think of was that his prompt action had saved the lives of Liesl's brother and myself, at a dreadful cost to himself, and it was up to us to repay this debt.

Joseph did not want to be left alone with the injured man, and since I knew that we would probably need each other's help to find our way up the desolate mountain face, back to the safe route we knew, I agreed to let him come with me.

I made Niall as comfortable as possible and left a note, where he could not miss seeing it if he recovered consciousness, telling him that we had gone for help, and very slowly, very cautiously we crept from the cave and inched our way up and over the broken mountainside.

It must have taken us well over two hours to reach what I considered the safety line, although we still had quite a bit to go before we attained the actual track.

My watch had been broken when Niall had pushed me into the ⊦ nnel, and the hands still pointed to half past eleven. It must be well after two o'clock now, I judged. Surely Liesl, or her parents, would wonder about us? I had promised to be back with Joseph in plenty of time for lunch in order not to hold up the preparations for the wedding reception, so surely, Liesl, at least, knowing I was a stickler for punctuality, must guess something had gone wrong and have the sense to send someone to look out for us.

It wasn't Liesl, but Jon Crispin, who had been worried by our non-return. As we stumbled wearily down the track, we met him coming up.

The moment I saw him, I ran towards him and he cried out, "Miranda!" and ran to meet me.

I clung to him, half crying, half laughing, with weak hysteria.

"My darling!" He held me close, as he had

held me after yesterday's accident, strongly, tenderly, soothingly.

"Miranda! Please, my dearest. You look all in! What has happened?"

For a few seconds, I did not answer. I felt so safe in his embrace I did not want to pull myself away to tell him how Joseph's "secret" and his curiosity had nearly been the death of us, and how one more villain was dead, and another lay alone and dying.

Even Liesl's brother was too exhausted and near to collapse to speak, so that, in the end, Jon had to push me away, hold me at arm's length and shake me sternly back to my senses.

Somehow I managed to pull myself together and tell him our fantastic story as, with his arm round my waist, he helped me down the hillside.

He never once interrupted, but when we reached the belt of pine trees, where the mountain slope became less steep, he lifted me up in his arms, and telling Joseph to hurry ahead and ask his step-father to come and meet us, he carried me towards the Gasthof; I was too tired and weary, and grateful, too, to protest at being treated like a baby.

Chapter Twenty-two

Herr Katz met us as we were leaving the wood.

"What is this wild story Joseph has made up!" he demanded angrily.

"It isn't a story, Herr Katz," I protested. "It is the truth."

Katz's eyes looked from me to Jon.

"Try and get hold of some men, Herr Katz," Jon spoke briskly. "We shall have to hurry to reach Paterson and bring him back here before nightfall. Joseph will be able to tell you how to reach the place, when you are making your arrangements."

"My poor Liesl thought her troubles were at an end," groaned Katz. "Today, for the first time since I married her mother, she has been herself again, so happy with her friends and so excited at preparing this reception for Rosa!"

He hesitated. "Do we need to disturb the wedding guests?"

"I should imagine Herr Braun and Herr Werner will be willing to give us a hand. Perhaps one of your farm workers, too. That should be enough," Jon spoke quickly. "Also, we shall have to telephone Inspector Bauer and tell him what has happened."

"I shall attend to all these things," said Katz promptly.

"Good!" Jon nodded. "Meantime, I shall take Fräulein MacIntosh to her room and have a word with your wife. I shall rejoin you in a few minutes."

Katz nodded and Jon carried me up to my bedroom and laid me gently on the bed.

"There, my silly child! I have to leave you now, but before I go, promise me you will take a hot bath to ease your scrapes and bruises, some hot soup to refresh you, and," he smiled at me, "put on a pretty dress to greet me when I finally manage to get back to the Gasthof!"

He bent down and kissed me swiftly on the forehead, and then he was gone, so quickly that I hadn't time to answer him, but as I painfully removed my torn and dusty clothing and lay in a hot bath, perfumed with fragrant verbena, to soak my aches away, I could not think of the grim tragedy which had been enacted on the Schwarzberg for thinking of the look in a man's eyes, as he held me firmly in his arms; and the tenderness of a man's kiss of farewell, and because it seemed impossible to me that a man of the world like Jon Crispin, with his reputation for dallying only with very beautiful and sophisticated women, should look at me like that, I told myself I had imagined his expression.

All the same, as I patted myself dry and dressed, slowly and carefully, in a dress of soft, peridot green wool, which was cosy and yet did not irritate the bruises on my back and shoulders, I could not help thinking of Jon and wistfully wishing I was more glamorous and worldly.

After I brushed out my hair and put on some make-up, I went downstairs to the kitchen, where Liesl's mother was waiting to give both

Joseph and me a deliciously filling dumpling
soup, beef olives and, for me at least, coffee laced
with brandy.

Joseph had told her of our adventure, but
once she was satisfied I was none the worse for
it, she refrained from reminding me of it and did
not ask the many questions which must have
been on her mind.

After the meal, I went back to my bedroom to
watch, from the window, the wedding reception
of Liesl's friend, Rosa. In view of the lovely day,
it was being held outside, with a long table set
out in the orchard, covered with a snow-white
cloth and decorated with epergnes of mountain
flowers and the Gasthof's very best china and
cutlery.

Although from time to time I couldn't help
wondering if poor Niall was still alive, and if the
rescue party had reached him yet, and if so, how
soon they would arrive back at the Gasthof, the
merry scene below helped to take my mind off
the tragedy, and also helped to lighten the hours
of waiting.

I sat at my window until the reception was
over, and even after that I sat on, looking out on
the valley and the mountains, while the air grew
chill and darkness fell, and the first stars began
to twinkle in the heavens.

Then, with nightfall, I grew restless and went
downstairs to the parlour bar, where some of the
wedding guests, who had stayed on, were beginning to start up a merry sing-song.

In half an hour, dinner would be served.

I wondered how much longer it would be before the rescuers returned.

Irma Werner looked into the parlour and signalled to me.

"My husband and the others have newly returned," she told me. "I think Mr. Crispin is looking for you."

"Oh!" My heart gave an excited flutter as I thanked her and went to find Jon.

He was standing at the front door, talking to Katz. The moment he saw me, he excused himself to Liesl's step-father and came to me. He took my arm and led me out to the garden.

"Paterson is dead," he told me without preamble. "He died as we were carrying him down the mountainside."

A tear trickled down my cheek.

Poor Niall. Whatever wrongs he had done, and whatever wrongs he had planned to do, he had died in saving me.

"Paterson wasn't worth your emotion!" said Jon harshly.

"He saved my life," I said simply.

"His one moment of weakness. He was a ruthless, ambitious man." Jon looked at me. "Yet it seems that somehow you moved him to some kindlier feelings, Miranda. You have a way of insinuating yourself into a man's heart, my dear." His fingers entwined mine and held them firmly, as he went on:

"Do you know who and what Paterson was?"

I shook my head.

"You guessed nothing?"

Again, I shook my head.

As we strolled on, out past the orchard into the moonwashed meadow, Jon whistled a tune.

"Do you recognize that?"

"Yes!" I stopped and stared at him. "That was the tune Heinrich whistled when he killed Schneider—and again today!"

"It is the Horst Wessel Lied, Miranda. The marching song of the old Nazi party. Your Niall was one of the new Nazis. In fact, he was the nephew of the man nominated by Adolf Hitler, before he killed himself, to take over the leadership of the party should anything happen to Martin Bormann."

"Jon! I don't understand!"

"It's a long story, my dear. Paterson told us bits and pieces of it as we lifted him over the landslide. The rest we have pieced together from rumours rampant in this area; rumours which Inspector Bauer has been interested in for some time.

"Your dream castle, Rohrdorf, Miranda, has been for years the secret hideout of Bormann's successor!

"While Europe and Asia and South America have been searched in vain for him, he has been sitting pretty in his mountain hideout, where only a handful of the faithful knew of the secret tunnel which led to the castle—a tunnel made by the remnants of the garrison which was cut off in 1945!

"Heinrich, the barman, was one of these men and he was in a good position to procure provisions and other things which the leader required. Heinrich was such a familiar figure on the mountains—he and his two friends who worked in Schwarzberg itself, that no one thought anything of their constant forays up the hillside.

"If anyone looked like finding the tunnel, they met with an unfortunate 'accident' to keep the secret safe. That is what happened to Schneider.

"You can guess when Schneider's death was mooted to be murder, the Nazi cell was driven to desperate methods to stop awkward questions being asked, and they had no compunction in ridding themselves of awkward witnesses!

"They were afraid Rudi had mentioned Heinrich's name to Hans; afraid also that you might have heard one address another by name when you overheard the murder, and remembered this at a future date, even if you hadn't mentioned it to begin with—"

"But, Jon!" I protested. "If Niall was involved in all this why was he so anxious to get me out of the country yesterday? He really intended to take me to Munich and put me on the London 'plane."

"That was a reasonable move. Once you were out of Austria, you were out of the way of further questioning! You were never likely to come back, and moreover, my dear, you underestimate your charms! For all his talk of choosing a wife by computer, I believe Paterson was genuinely attracted to you."

"I know!" I shivered, and Jon's clasp on my hand tightened. "He told Heinrich he need only kill Joseph, since he was going to marry me and would see I kept a still tongue in my head.

"Jon! Tell me. How did an Englishman get mixed up with these Nazis?"

"Paterson wasn't English," stated Jon. "It seems his mother, a sister of the present 'leader', whom the police hope to arrest tonight, acquired a Dutch passport at the end of the war, married an English officer in the occupation army, and returned with him and her eight-year-old son to England. There, although his English step-father knew nothing of it, his mother brought him up to admire Hitler and his works. She knew her brother was still alive and she hoped her son would be given a place of importance in the Neo Nazi Party!"

Jon stopped speaking and we walked slowly on through the meadow.

"Tomorrow, Miranda," he spoke again, "Inspector Bauer is coming to ask you a few questions, to corroborate the facts he has learned. After that," he turned to look at me, "try to forget all that has happened here this week, or if you do remember it at times, make believe it was all a bad dream."

I stared ahead of me.

Drifting cobwebs floated against my face. The night was full of a thousand noises, of whispering wind, and unseen insects, or fly-by-night birds and swooping bats.

The mountains around us rose, high and austere, their snow caps crystal bright in the starlight, the pine belts casting mysterious shadows on their moon silvered flanks.

There was a feeling of timelessness and serenity, beauty and peace in the scene.

"Jon!" I cried out in bitterness. "Why does man have to spoil things! Why did Niall opt for a part in power politics and racialism? He seemed so pleasant and conventional. He was clever and intelligent and handsome! He could have made so much of his life."

"You were fond of him, weren't you, Miranda?"

"He seemed so nice," I said sadly. "But then, it seems I am not a very good judge of men!" I gave him a shamefaced smile.

"Do you know, to begin with I didn't like you at all! I thought you were hard and cynical and—and—" my voice trailed off.

"And what?" Jon stopped, unclasped his hand from mine and lifted up my chin, so that I was forced to look directly into his eyes.

"And—and a man who fancied himself as a lady killer," I said in a low voice, and lowered my gaze.

"I'm sorry, Jon," I said gruffly.

"Sorry for what, Miranda?"

"Sorry because—oh, please, Jon, let me be—" I tried to pull away from him, but still he forced me to look at him.

"Sorry because you found out that, after all, I was none of these things?" His voice was teasing. "Sorry, because yesterday I kissed you as if you were a woman?" his voice grew harsher. "Sorry, Miranda, because you have made me fall in love with you?"

His fingers were on my arms, gripping them so

tightly I winced and tried to pull away, but he held me the more firmly.

"Miranda, my dear," his voice was pleading. "Stop trying to run away from me! You were glad enough to run to my arms when you needed me this afternoon, and yesterday."

I couldn't believe what his words implied!

"You told me I must forget everything that has happened this week!" I protested breathlessly, my pulse racing.

"You little witch!"

He shook me angrily. "Don't play with me! Tell me, do you want to forget me? Have you no thought of me as other than a convenient pair of arms to comfort you when there was no one else around to give comfort?"

I could not meet his irate eyes.

"Go on!" he urged. "Tell me, Miranda, do you want to forget me, too? Am I always to be merely part of a bad dream?"

I could not trust my voice. How could I tell this man what he had grown to mean to me? How could I put into words what I felt for him? How could I explain the unexplainable, that since the moment of our first meeting I had felt all too strongly attracted to him.

I raised my eyes to look at him, and the stars in their depths were not reflected from the sky.

"Oh, Jon, my darling!" I whispered.

"Miranda!"

I don't know who moved towards who—I was in Jon's arms, he was in mine, and he was looking down at me in that way which melted my bones.

"Once upon a time, my darling girl, you quoted Donne to me," he rubbed his cheek against mine. "Now, let me quote him to you, even if the lines from 'The Bait' are a mere echo of Marlowe!"

His lips were soft on my hair, my forehead, my temples, my cheek.

" 'Come live with me, and be my love,' darling, darling Miranda!" he whispered.

I let out a little shuddering sigh of happiness before he kissed me full on the lips, with passion, for the second time in our lives.

This time, I did not run away!

Wyndham Books are obtainable from many booksellers and newsagents. If you have any difficulty please send purchase price plus postage on the scale below to:

Wyndham Cash Sales,
123 King Street,
London W6 9JG

OR

Star Book Service,
G.P.O. Box 29,
Douglas,
Isle of Man,
British Isles

While every effort is made to keep prices low, it is sometimes necessary to increase prices at short notice. Wyndham Books reserve the right to show new retail prices on covers which may differ from those advertised in the text or elsewhere.

Postage and Packing Rate
U.K. & Eire
One book 15p plus 7p per copy for each additional book ordered to a maximum charge of 57p.

These charges are subject to Post Office charge fluctuations.